TROUBLEMAKER

A DARK COLLEGE HOCKEY ROMANCE

TABB U
BOOK 2

JO BRENNER

Editing provided by Emily McNish (@EmilyintheArchives)

Cover design provided by Notorious Cover Designs.

For everyone who wonders if a whistle can be used as a sex toy...

Daddy Coach will show you how to blow it.

ALSO BY JO BRENNER

Bad Heroes
>You Can Follow Me
>Lose Me In The Shadows
>Meet Me In The Dark

Tabb U
>Butterfly: a dark college hockey romance

Kings of Reina University
>Brutal Game: a dark college hockey romance
>Heartless Game: a dark college hockey romance

PLAYLIST

Man of the Year
Lorde
When Did You Get Hot?
Sabrina Carpenter
Blue Strips
Jessie Murph
Impossible
James Arthur
thank u, next
Ariana Grande
My Man on Willpower
Sabrina Carpenter
Young Dumb & Broke
Khalid
About Damn Time
Lizzo
Good as Hell (feat. Ariana Grande)
Lizzo
Fuck You
Lily Allen

Jackie and Wilson

Hozier

Burning Down

Alex Warren

Too Sweet

Hozier

Unholy

Sam Smith & Kim Petras

Lose Control

Teddy Swims

drivers license

Olivia Rodrigo

come out and play

Billie Eilish

Skinny Love (cover)

Birdy

SECRET LOVER

Chad Walt

Sugar Talking

Sabrina Carpenter

Shove It (feat. Spank Rock)

Santigold

Bad Girls

MKTO

Better

Khalid

The Love Club

Lorde

She Is

The Fray

Take Me To Church

Hozier

Slow Burn

Sadie Jean
Say Something
A Great Big World & Christina Aguilera
I'll Be Good
Jaymes Young

IMPORTANT CONTENT NOTE

Content Note! Please Read

This is a dark, taboo romance, with dark themes and plot points that may be sensitive to some.

Please, please, please read the content warnings on my website, jobrenner.com. I'd add them here, but the River Platform (IYKYK) could get big mad if it sees the list, and then bye bye, book.

Joking aside, please do visit my website. Your health—mental, physical, spiritual, emotional—matters.

AUTHOR'S NOTE

When *Butterfly* came out, I mentioned in the author's note that I wrote it in a literal fever dream (I had Covid at the time). This may seem insignificant, but I—and many readers, based on the DMs and emails I got—were convinced I'd have to get severely ill again to write Coach and Lucy's story.

And Coach and Lucy's story is by far my most asked for book.

When I first came up with their characters, I loved Lucy at first dialogue. Spunky, beautiful, witty, and absolutely unapologetic in who she was, Lucy was who I wanted to be when I grew up. Coach, then, had to be repressed (sorry: "controlled and controlling"), pissed the fuck off at everyone and anyone, and absolutely smitten with her as an adult. They had to challenge each other: Coach had to teach Lucy that she could take off the armor every so often (because all that pink *is* armor, against a world that didn't want her or value her). And Lucy had to teach Coach it was okay for him to let go and be himself, that he wasn't a terrible man underneath it all.

Still, after *Butterfly*, I worried. I didn't actually want to get sick again (although some of you joked about it), but I wasn't sure if I wasn't in a completely delusional mental state, I'd be able to write Coach and Lucy the way I needed to.

And then 2025 happened.

I could get into the ways that this year has broken me—broken a lot of us—but I need a moment of levity, so I'll leave that be. Suffice it to say, what I needed *was* levity, and joy, and some utter filthy nonsense as two unhinged people fell in love. And maybe to explore the parts of myself—the parts of ourselves—who desperately need to learn it's okay to let go of our armor in this world...to let go, period.

So that's what I wrote. Filthy nonsense, and two unhinged people falling in love and finding happiness in a world that desperately needs it.

I hope you enjoy.

Love,

Jo

PROLOGUE
LUCY

When I was seven years old, I fell in love.

He was tall—almost a giant—with dark hair, eyes so dark green they were almost black, a square jaw, and a stern, serious look on his face—even back then.

He was one of my father's hockey players. See, Elijah Braverman owned...well, he owned a lot of things when he was still alive. But one of those things was The Gehenom Beasts: our city's NHL team. And on that day—the day I fell in love—at my seventh birthday party, the whole team had come to celebrate with me. Supposedly. Really, it was because they had to.

My mother had left me with a somber black dress and pointy, uncomfortable black flats. I didn't understand why I couldn't wear the pink dress I'd picked out, or why she wanted my birthday to feel like a funeral. But then Anastasia Braverman always preferred when I wore black, probably because I could blend in better with the uniformed staff that way. She never cared. If she had, she wouldn't have ordered the chef to make a carrot cake for my birthday cake.

I was allergic to carrots.

So I was in a sad little black dress and painful shoes, sulking over not being able to have my own birthday cake, when I first saw *him*.

His name was Blake Samson. He was twenty-five. Based on the way the other players teased him, he took himself *way* too seriously. And he, of course, didn't notice the child whose birthday it was—until I tripped over my own uncomfortable shoes and fell on the grass, scraping my knee.

I felt like a baby, but it hurt, and I was embarrassed, so I cried.

My parents were nowhere in sight—probably at some business meeting disguised as party fun—and almost everyone ignored me. Birthday girl or not, they were here to suck up to my dad, not his only child. I was an afterthought to everyone, like usual.

Except Blake. He spotted me crying, curled up on the ground, sad, lonely, and hurting. And he walked over to me and knelt down on the grass, ignoring the way it stained his pants.

"You okay, kid?" he asked gruffly.

I nodded, not wanting to show how pitiful I felt. But Blake must have seen through it, because with a small, knowing smile, he shook his head.

"No, you're not. Let me look at that knee."

"I didn't know hockey players could be doctors," I said. It probably came off rude, but I was hurting and not used to someone paying attention to my pain. I didn't trust it.

Instead of getting defensive, he shrugged. "Nah, but I've seen my fair share of cuts and bruises."

It seemed like a weird thing to say, but maybe it was because hockey was such a "violent sport," like my mother always said. I would've asked Blake, but he was too busy looking at my knee, like it was a serious injury.

He glanced at me. "Tell you what, it looks like a bad scrape. I'm going to go get some stuff to clean it up. Wait here."

He disappeared for a few minutes, then reappeared with a first aid kit.

"I keep it in my car," he said at the question in my eyes, squatting down. He still towered over me. Carefully, with the precision of a surgeon, he cleaned out the cut, apologizing for the sting, before placing a bandage over it.

"There you go, kid," he said. "Should be all better." Then he spotted my fingers. I always bit my nails, which my parents hated, but it was one of the few things that calmed me down when I was anxious or sad.

"Why do you bite your nails?"

"Um..." I hesitated, feeling shy.

"You know, I used to bite my nails, too. Whenever I got scared, or lonely. But instead, I came up with something that didn't mess with them. Do you want to know what it was?"

"What?" I was curious and entranced by his kind face.

"I tell myself stories. No matter how silly, I tell myself stories with happy endings and it makes the bad feelings go away. You should try it."

"Thanks," I said, feeling shy.

He shrugged. "Anytime. Stay out of trouble from now on, okay?"

And with that, he was gone—and I was head over heels.

♥.♥

AFTER THAT, I ALWAYS NOTICED BLAKE—AT GAMES, AT DINNER at my house, or when he came over and he and my father would disappear into his office. My dad started referring to him as the "son he'd never had." I was never allowed to have meals with my parents because I was too loud and messy, but whenever Blake came over, I'd watch from the doorway of the kitchen. My dad was warm with him in a way he never was with me, and if Blake had been a jerk, I would've hated him for it.

But Blake always made sure to visit me in the kitchen before he left, patting me on the head, calling me kid, and asking me how school was. I was too young to realize how starved I was for attention, because even those brief moments made him the kindest person I knew.

I was twelve when my parents died. Their private plane had crashed on their way to some vacation somewhere. I hadn't been with them because they never brought me along, and I guess, in that way, I was lucky.

On the day of the funeral, I stood alone in the first row of the synagogue. I had no aunts and uncles, no cousins, no living grandparents, leaving my father's lawyer to plan the funeral. The rows behind me were filled, but aside from awkward hugs from my father's employees and work friends, no one bothered to come close to me, to offer support or comfort. I was alone.

Then someone cleared their throat. I turned and looked up.

Blake stood there in a black suit. He seemed older, gruffer, almost stiff, pulling at the tie around his neck like it didn't belong there.

"I'm sorry for your loss," he said. He looked lost, himself. "I think I'm supposed to say, 'May their memories be a blessing,' right?"

I nodded, forcing a smile on my face, although all I wanted was a hug.

"Yeah."

"This is a stupid question, but how are you doing?"

I shrugged. "Okay."

But I couldn't stop the tears from falling. I hadn't been close to my parents, but they were all I had, and now it was just me.

The stiffness in Blake's body softened. He opened his arms and hugged me. For the first time that I could remember, I felt safe.

"You don't have to be okay," he told me. "You can be however you want to be."

He stayed near me during the service and the burial, and even though it was probably just pity, it didn't feel that way. He even rode with me back to the house for the shiva—when everyone came over to "mourn" with me like you do in Jewish tradition—but was pulled away by various people who wanted to talk to him.

So when my parents' lawyer asked me to come upstairs to my dad's office to hear about the will, what my parents had left me, and who they had left me to, I was surprised to see Blake there.

I was extra surprised when he couldn't look me in the eye.

"Lucy, your parents left you everything in a trust—except for the team, which the estate sold, as per their instructions in the will."

I nodded, feeling numb. I was twelve. I didn't really care about the money, or any of it, because I was too young to understand just how rich I was. I just wanted to know where I was going to be living, and who I was going to be living with. Someone needed to take care of me.

"Lucy, you do have a guardian. Your parents trusted Blake Samson—your father specifically said he 'loved him like a son.' So they left you to him in their will." Pity in his eyes, he added, "There was no one else."

I ignored the way the words 'loved him like a son,' hurt. My parents had never told me they loved me. I was too busy replaying the last sentence, the shock of it...and the hope.

Maybe my parents, as much as they hadn't cared, had cared a little...because even if there really was no one else, they still left me to someone who was kind.

I glanced over at Blake. He still wouldn't look at me.

"Did you know?" I asked.

He jerked his head once in a nod.

The lawyer sighed. "Lucy, Blake has decided, appropriately, that you should go to boarding school until you turn eighteen, when you can go off to college."

Boarding school.

Not with him.

Alone.

Even more alone than I'd been.

The hope I'd felt started to slip away.

"Blake," I said, my voice small as I tried not to cry.

Blake finally looked at me.

"I'm sorry, kid," he said. "This is the best thing for you."

As he turned to go, any bit of hope that still lingered inside me died.

That was the last I saw of him. Blake never bothered to see me, never wrote me back when I wrote him, never returned my calls. It was like he'd never existed.

That's when I learned there wasn't much to be in love with, after all.

Because love was for foolish little girls who thought a small gesture of kindness meant everything.

And I wasn't a foolish little girl.
Not anymore.

SIX YEARS LATER

1

LUCY

From: blake.samson@tabb.edu

To: idowhatiwant@tabb.edu

Lucy,

See me in my office at 9 a.m.

On the dot.

- Coach Samson

PS: I still can't believe they let you change your goddamn email address.

I seethed at the short, terse, scolding email from my cold and distant tyrant of a guardian. At the ripe young age of eighteen, and as a college freshman who often got into trouble—intentionally—Coach Blake Samson thought I was an immature dumbass. An immature dumbass who not only couldn't fight her way out of a paper bag but had fought her way in there in the first place. What he couldn't seem to understand was that I'd been taking care of myself since I was twelve years old, when my parents died, and he completely abandoned me. I might be immature, but I was the furthest thing from a dumbass, and I was getting—

"—so fucking sick and so fucking tired of him trying to boss me around!" I ranted to my best friend, Leslie, as we stood at the counter in our dorm's common bathroom, Leslie brushing her teeth as I added layer after layer of mascara. It was only 8:30 a.m., way too early for party girl makeup, but I knew it would piss Blake off...like being late would.

Next to me, Leslie paused in brushing her teeth to raise an eyebrow.

"So you say..." she hummed, mouth full of toothpaste.

"I mean it!" I argued, but I caught my faint blush in the mirror. Being blonde and pale really did me a disservice when it came to hiding my feelings, damn it.

"And if he bossed you around in the bedroom?" Leslie asked.

It sounded like, "An' i' e' bosh you arou' in the behroom," because of said mouthful of toothpaste, and usually I'd tease her for talking with her mouth full...and add a joke about how her mouth was usually full of her fiancé Mason's dick, but I was too annoyed to be on my usual game.

"Girl, I'm over that," I declared. "Maybe once upon a time I wanted to know what it would be like to be forced over his lap while he taught me a lesson, but that ship sailed loooooong ago. Besides, being bossed around in bed is your thing, not mine," I added.

Now it was Leslie's turn to blush. "You're such a liar," she accused. "I might like Mason's dominance, but you're into that stuff, too."

She was right. I might have been a virgin, but I had access to online porn and smutty romance books, same as the next person. *And* I'd fooled around a bit with college boys over the past few months...but it was always a huge disappointment. Maybe it was because I never let them take my clothes off, but whenever I got that far, whenever I *tried,* Blake's pissed-off face appeared in my mind, and I couldn't go through with it.

Just one more reason to hate him.

And even though my friend had somehow found a fiancé that knew his way around a pair of handcuffs, every other guy my age out there was a bumbling idiot when it came to sex—forceful or otherwise. They might pretend they could boss me around, but really, they were babies with boners. I needed a man.

But not Coach Samson, I reminded myself. Oh no, I'd find myself an older man, but it wouldn't be the asshole who was still in control of my life.

First, I had to finish getting ready and go get lectured by my guardian for whatever perceived trouble I had caused this time.

At least I'd get there late.

I applied Barbie Pink lipstick and blew myself a kiss.

There. I'd full-on piss him off.

"Have fun!" Leslie giggled as I turned to go in my low-rise jeans and tiny pink crop top, tugging it down for maximum cleavage—and I *had* a maximum.

"Oh, I will," I promised, because no matter how annoying the lecture was, I'd make sure to have fun...at "Coach's" expense.

I always did.

♥.♥

Tabb's campus was small and modern. No creeping ivy or gothic buildings. Tabb prided itself on being fully immersed in the present day, and that meant chrome, glass, and very little greenery. As I walked, a little part of my chest hurt, knowing that I'd originally wanted to go to Reina—the beautiful Ivy League university that rose on top of the hill as if it were looking down and judging us. Reina had a better veterinary sciences program, better everything, really. But it didn't have Blake Samson, and when I received my acceptance letters, that had been all that mattered to me. Although people thought I was "slutty and stupid" (a teacher at my boarding school had even called me that once), I was neither. I'd had perfect grades and SAT scores, and I was academically ambitious.

If it weren't for Leslie's friendship, I would've regretted my decision. As it was, my chest ached a little when I thought about it.

But it was fine.

Everything was fine.

I stared at my phone, playing with the ends of my long, blonde, wavy hair, letting 9 a.m. become 9:01, then 9:02.

Finally, at 9:07, I sauntered into the administration building, up the stairs to the athletics department, past the assistant coach as he called after me, "Lucy, why are you always late? He's going to be—" and pushed the door open to Coach Samson's office without knocking.

"You know, it is customary to wait for an invitation to enter someone's space," Coach said dryly as I crossed my arms and tilted my head back to stare up at him.

Even though I was 5'7", he towered over me...like he had when I was a little kid with a crush.

Don't think about that, I scolded myself.

"Why? I'm not a vampire," I shot back.

"Sit," he said, nodding to a chair in front of his big desk. A desk I'd fantasized about bending over more than once.

Ugh.

I hated that Leslie was right.

"I think I'll stand," I said.

He shrugged. "If these little moments of rebellion bring you joy, who am I to challenge them?"

Motherfucker.

I sat.

He laughed.

Damn it, how did he always manipulate me so easily?

He kept laughing, low in his throat, as I tried not to stare. His dark hair always fell over one eye, and I was always tempted to brush it back—like I'm sure every other person he came into contact with thought about doing. Coach had chiseled cheekbones, a flat nose, big dark eyes with obnoxiously long lashes, and a full mouth. He was still the giant he'd always been, easily 6'6", broad and muscular, dominating every space he entered and swallowing up all the air in the room. He looked like Captain America...if Captain America was always picturing ways to kill you.

Well, me. When Coach looked at me, it was like he'd swallowed sour milk at the exact same time someone shoved a broken hockey stick up his ass.

"Why am I here, Blake?" I snapped.

He immediately stopped laughing.

"The dean told me you got caught last weekend gorge jumping over at Reina U."

It was true. Reina had a much prettier campus than we had, with several gorges that drunk or high students would dare each other to jump into in the warmer months. I'd dragged Leslie there while Coach, and Mason, our center, were at an away game, and convinced our friends Tovah and

Aviva to join us. Sure, it was risky, but it was *fun*—until campus security caught us.

Clearing his throat, Blake added, "And that you were all naked."

That also was true. We'd given the security guard a real show.

Shit.

Blake reached for a glass of water on his desk and took a large gulp.

"I'm hardly the first Tabb student to partake in recreational water sports," I argued.

Blake choked on his water, spluttering. It spilled all over his pristine white button down, making the shirt stick to his chest. Girls on campus whispered that Coach had a better body than any of the players on the team, and with the way his shirt clung to his muscles, I could see it. I could *always* see it.

Blake was still choking on his water. I replayed the last thing I said, not sure why he—

Oh. *Water sports.*

I didn't have to see myself in a mirror this time to know I'd gone bright red. I usually was able to hide when I was embarrassed, except for when Coach was watching. Then, I lost any ability to control my reactions. It made me feel vulnerable, and I hated it. *Hated it.*

"That's not what I meant." This time, I was the one to splutter.

Recovering, Blake swallowed. God, even his throat was sexy. I hated him so fucking much. Why couldn't he be ugly?

"I have no idea what you possibly could have meant," Blake said smoothly. "What I do know is that I had to argue with the dean to keep him from putting you and your friend

Leslie on probation. You're lucky. Not only could you have lost your place at Tabb, you could have *died*."

I crossed my arms over my chest. "People gorge jump all the time!"

"And get hurt all the time. If I can't trust you to take care of yourself, Lucy..." he trailed off.

"Then what? What are you going to do to me, *Coach*?" That fantasy of being forced over his lap appeared in my head briefly before I banished it.

His eyes darkened for a moment, brushing over my body, and if I didn't know better, I'd think he was checking me out. I shivered from his indiscernible expression.

"You don't want to know, Lucy. That, I can promise," he said, voice thick.

He cleared his throat again. I wanted to believe it was because he was so taken with me and his own fantasies he could barely speak, but like I said, I knew better. The only fantasies Coach had of me were of me disappearing from his life forever, so he didn't have to feel responsible for me anymore. He'd certainly made that clear over the past six years.

He wasn't done. "From now on, you have a curfew. You will text me where you are, at *all* times. You will go to class, the library, the cafeteria, and back to your dorm room, where you will stay, all night, by *yourself*. No more parties, no more causing mayhem. No more trouble. Period."

I snorted. There was no way he could enforce that. I'd be more careful from now on. No one was going to control my actions or my life, least of all *him*.

"Yes, sir," I said sweetly, bending low in a curtsy...and making sure to flash him a bit of cleavage. I couldn't help myself.

His eyes remained on my face like he hadn't even noticed.

"Don't call me sir," he said. "You haven't earned the privilege. Now, get out of my office. You have class."

"Why do you know my schedule?" I asked.

"Because it's my duty to know everything about you, troublemaker," he said.

His *duty.*

Not because he cared.

Because he was still being dutiful to my long-dead father.

Well, he could shove his *duty* up his ass right next to that hockey stick.

I had mayhem to make and trouble to plan, after all.

I turned to go, already plotting. What was my first move? I guessed I could figure out how to melt the ice in the rink...

"Oh, and Lucy," he added. "I had to make a deal with the dean to keep you in good academic standing. You'll be volunteering."

"I already volunteer," I said. I worked at the Gehenom animal shelter two nights a week. Even though I wasn't a vet yet, I did what I could to help.

"More volunteering," he said. "Not the type that's connected to your major."

Dread filled my stomach. He sounded too satisfied; I could hear the smirk in his voice.

"Where?" I asked.

"With the hockey team."

Fuck.

Me.

But I wasn't about to let him win.

Turning back around, I twirled my hair and looked at him from under my lashes.

"That's fine," I said. "I've had my eye on some of the players, anyway. This will just give me a chance to know them better."

With that, I swayed my hips as I made my way out of his office without saying another word, opening the office door and slamming it on his animalistic growl.

As I sashayed out of the office, I winked at his assistant.

"See you later, Trey," I trilled, knowing his eyes were on my ass.

"You're just making our lives harder," he called after me.

I giggled. "Who's hard?"

Trey sighed. "That mouth is going to get you in trouble one of these days."

"I hope so," I said.

I did hope so.

As long as it was the *right* kind of trouble.

2

BLAKE

I was a good man. I *tried* to be a good man. Paid my taxes, devoted myself to my players and my team, donated to foster care-related charities, mentored orphans just like I'd been mentored all those years ago. I was in control of myself and everything and everyone around me, and that was how I liked it.

I needed to be in control of myself. I'd never known my own parents, but all the adult caregivers I had known were drunk and abusive foster parents who probably couldn't even spell control. I'd been big, even as a kid, so they usually picked on foster siblings and not me. But I was the only protection my foster siblings had, so I'd put myself in the way, letting myself get beat on until I was big enough to do the beating myself.

Which was why I got moved around so much. Fortunately, one of said abusive foster parents had been a hockey coach, so I'd gotten my first introduction to the ice at a young age. And after I moved out of that home, I lucked out *again,* because my mentor in the Big Brothers Big Sisters program owned his own damn hockey team. He saw to it that I got training.

That man was none other than Elijah Braverman, Lucy's father.

Elijah seemed like a cold man to everyone but me. He'd told me I reminded him of himself, and so he'd taken me under his wing, regularly invited me to his home, and treated me like he was the father I'd never had. Before they'd died in that freak accident, Elijah shared that they were leaving Lucy to me in the will, "just in case." It had made me uncomfortable at the time.

"Why?" I'd asked him.

"Lucy's a tricky kid. She's too needy for most people. But you seem to tolerate her well enough, so you're our best option. Don't worry; if we do die, there's plenty of money and you can always ship her off to boarding school."

He'd laughed, and I'd had to stop myself from retorting that Lucy didn't seem needier than any other young kid. The whole thing made me uncomfortable, but since he'd given me everything and made my dreams possible, I couldn't deny him that. Plus, there was no way in the world they'd die. This was all hypothetical.

Until it wasn't.

God, Lucy.

She was the one thing in my life I always tried to exert control over—only to fail.

She was also why I was going to hell.

Eighteen years old, 40% golden curls and siren curves, 60% dynamite, and as off-limits as a woman could get. It hadn't been an issue before, of course. Back when Elijah had been alive, I'd barely noticed her at all, other than as my boss's sweet, chaotic, overlooked kid. And then after he and his wife died, I just saw her as a motherfucking pain-in-the-ass responsibility. I sent her off to boarding school like he'd recommended because what the hell did I know about raising a teenager? I had no parental figures in my own life; I certainly wasn't going to be an exemplary version of one. No, better that she get a good education, far away from me.

And then she showed up at orientation, and she wasn't a gawky, chatty, grieving kid anymore with blonde frizzy hair and braces. No, she was barely recognizable: A tall, built woman with curves for days, long, wavy blonde hair that made a bad man want to wrap it around his hand and tug hard, dark bedroom eyes and big pouty lips that...fuck, I couldn't even go there.

If that weren't enough, she was loud, confident, fucking funny as hell, and so sassy that a man would want to put her over his knee and turn her ass red for it until she was crying and saying, *sorry, daddy, I'll be better, I promise—*

She was unholy temptation in a short dress and pink lips, and the second I saw her, I knew she'd be trouble.

The devil in a tight dress.

A motherfucking succubus.

And none of it was her fault. All of it was mine.

After our first pre-season hockey game, she'd come right up to me on the ice—not even caring that she wasn't supposed to *be* on the ice. Marched right up to me, smacked me on the shoulder, and said, "You don't write, you don't call. I'm starting to think you don't like me much, *Coach.*"

I'd blinked at the much-too-young-for-me goddess and said, "I'm sorry, I don't know who you are."

She'd snorted. "I guess I'm not surprised. I'm Lucy, your ward. The kid you used to be responsible for but fobbed off on expensive academic institutions. Except I'm all grown up now. Miss me?"

Alarm bells had begun to ring in my head, and disgust

filled me, because how the hell could I be attracted to my motherfucking ward? My one single responsibility, all grown up just like she'd said, and clearly here for blood.

And part of me, a dark, sick part of me, had wanted her to rake her fingers down my chest and make it bleed.

"Coach? Coach? *Blake*."

I shook my head to clear it. My assistant coach, Trey Putrovksi, was snapping his fingers in front of my face. We were in the middle of our weekly one-on-one to discuss the team, and I'd zoned out for most of it.

Because of Lucy fucking Braverman. She was goddamn kryptonite, put on this earth to destroy my head, my equilibrium, and make a good man go bad.

"Yeah, all that sounds great," I said. "Although I think we need to work more closely with Emory—he's been off his game lately, and I'm not sure why, but we need to get him back on it."

"Girl trouble," Trey snorted. "And the unfixable kind. He wants someone out of his reach and it's fucking with his head."

At my look, he added, "I'll take care of it. Speaking of girl trouble..."

Ah, shit.

I knew what this was about, and I apparently couldn't avoid it any longer.

I schooled my features into a concerned expression. "Hmm?"

"My sister Alison has been talking about you a lot lately. Said she gave you her number and you never called..." he rubbed his beard awkwardly, obviously not wanting to have this conversation with me.

"Yeah, sorry, I forgot. I've been too busy."

He raised a brow. "You forgot? Or you're just not interested?"

I wasn't interested. Not in the least. My dick only got hard for one woman, and she was the one woman I couldn't have.

"You never put yourself out there," he added. "Practically a monk. You know that's not good for you, right?"

"I'll call her," I said.

He nodded. "Good."

"Oh, one more item before we finish up. Lucy Braverman is going to be assisting the team for the rest of the season."

Trey's eyes widened. "The kid Elijah left to you in the will? The trust fund brat? The one who comes sashaying in and out of your office like she doesn't give two fucks about anything?"

My hands fisted underneath my desk. Lucy might be a brat, but no one could call her that but me. And yes, she had a trust fund, but she didn't have access to it until she was twenty-one...making her reliant on me financially for the next three years. I hated how much I loved that, knowing I was her sole provider.

"She's not a kid," I said, instead, a little defensively, causing Trey's eyes to go wider.

"Why are we bringing on someone who knows jack shit about hockey? Doesn't she want to be a veterinarian or something?"

"How do you know that?" Annoyance shot through me. Why was Trey even talking to Lucy?

He shrugged. "I think she mentioned it at some point. So what's going on?"

I sighed, rubbing a hand through my hair. "She's about

to get herself expelled. Doing unsafe shit. I need to keep a better eye on her."

"And you think bringing her to practices with a lot of horny hockey players is the way to keep her in line?"

When he put it that way, no, I didn't. What I wanted was to lock her up somewhere safe where she couldn't do reckless bullshit anymore, like a tower where only I had the key, or my bedroom...but that was a fucked-up thought that led to other, much more fucked-up thoughts.

"She'll stay busy, she'll stay out of trouble, and we'll make sure to make it clear to the entire team that it's a hands-off situation," I decided. "No looking, no touching, or you can say goodbye to playing for the rest of the season."

Trey coughed.

"What?"

"Nothing, just...very protective of you. Very...fatherly."

My stomach roiled. The very last goddamn thing in the world I felt toward the little troublemaker was fatherly. But that would have to remain a secret between me and my depraved cock.

One I'd take to the grave.

3

LUCY

"I hate him, I hate him, I hate him, I hate him so much," I said as I stomped into Mason and Leslie's condo later that day.

"That's a lot of 'I hate him's,'" Leslie said with a laugh from where she sat on Mason's lap.

Mason looked amused. But then Mason always looked amused when it came to me. I'd overheard him once tell Leslie that, even though he didn't like that I was a bad—and sometimes dangerous—influence on her (i.e., *slightly* reckless gorge jumping), he also appreciated that I'd influenced her to accept her feelings for him. So I was allowed to remain in her life "with supervision."

Leslie and I both said fuck it to supervision though. He might be a little bit of a stalker, but if Leslie wanted it, she got it—and she wanted to be friends with me.

Mason also knew *all* about Coach, and my previous crush on Coach, and my current hatred *for* Coach.

"You know," Mason said as he stroked a hand through Leslie's hair, "I once hated someone too. So much so, I lashed out at her for it."

"Like by coming in my ballet shoes?" Leslie asked pointedly.

He tugged on her hair. "Something like that."

"Well, as fun as it would be to desecrate something that's important to Coach, I don't think I want to come all over his whistle. Although..." I waved the idea away. "No, I'll find better ways to torture him."

"Like?" Leslie looked intrigued.

"Oh, I don't know," I said, as I mentally made a list of Ways to Make Blake Samson, He Who Never Loses His Shit, Lose His Shit. "I could show up to practice naked. I could take over the sound system and play Sabrina Carpenter—he *hates* Sabrina Carpenter. I could write 'Coach Samson Has A Tiny Penis' on the rink...can you write on ice? How do you dye ice?"

Mason opened his mouth to answer but I waved him off, on a roll. "I could fill his office with chickens. I could spend a practice teaching all of you the dance to 'Texas Hold 'Em.' I glanced at Mason. "Can you dance?"

He shrugged. "Probably."

"I'd like to see that," Leslie said.

"I'll give you a show later," he promised, kissing her, and I tried not to be distracted by my own yearning. Not because I wanted Mason. Far from it. Because I wanted someone in my life to look at me the way he looked at her, like she meant everything. Like if she asked him to set the world on fire, he'd immediately find a match. No one in my life had ever looked at me like I mattered to them, much less like I mattered more than anything or anyone else. When I let myself feel it, it was really fucking lonely...which is why I didn't.

And wouldn't right now.

Instead, I pulled out my phone and started typing up my list of ways to break Blake Samson and his tight grasp on his control, because if he was going to make me be at his beck and call for the rest of the season, if he was going to take away my freedom, I was going to make him regret it.

4

BLAKE

"Why the hell do I hear Sabrina Carpenter?" I snapped at Trey as we headed past the locker room and out through the tunnel onto the ice. The pop star's voice annoyed the crap out of me. Everyone on the team and the staff knew that. Someone was fucking with me.

I was in a bad enough mood as it was; the anticipation of seeing Lucy had made it impossible to sleep the night before, and my coffee maker had died this morning. I was tired, uncaffeinated, unfamiliarly antsy, and what's more, according to Lucy's RA—who I had paid off to keep an eye on her—Lucy didn't get back to her dorm room until midnight, completely disregarding the curfew that I'd imposed. Furthermore, she hadn't responded to any of my texts demanding she check in and show me proof that she was at home, safe and sound. The first chance I got, I was going to install a GPS tracker on her phone so I always knew where she was.

And the first person to piss me off today was going to get the figurative version of a blade to the neck.

When we reached the rink, I stopped short.

Lucy—in a short flippy pink skirt and a white top that revealed her entire lower back—was on skates, laughing, as Emory, the player Trey had claimed had girl trouble, pulled her along the ice.

Was Lucy the cause of his girl trouble?

Heat filled my stomach, the cue that I was about to lose my temper.

"You're doing great," he told her as he pulled her. "You're a natural."

"It's all you," she said sweetly. "I've always been too scared to go on the ice."

Bull fucking shit. Lucy had grown up on skates—she was as comfortable on the ice as I was. She was playing games with my team, and obviously with me.

Lifting my whistle to my lips, I blew it.

Emory released Lucy, who stumbled, making my heart catch in my throat. There was no way I could get to her in time...that ice would hurt, scrape up her bare legs...

...but she righted herself and spun around, looking at me with innocent eyes.

"Oh, should I not be on the ice, *Coach*?" she asked sweetly. "Your players were being such gentlemen, teaching me how to skate."

I couldn't respond to the minx, not with my tongue as dry as it was.

Because Lucy wasn't wearing a bra.

It was the most stunning, horrifying thing I'd ever seen. Her areolas darkened the fabric, pert little nipples pushing it out into points. They better have been hard because she was cold, and not because skating with Emory had turned her on.

I blew my whistle again.

"Ms. Braverman, come over here and take those skates off. I hired you to help the team by sweeping the ice during practices, gathering pucks, and bringing the team towels and water. Not for you to get free skating lessons."

I could feel her anger from across the ice.

"You didn't hire me to help, you hired me to babysit me," she pointed out, flipping her damn hair. To Emory, she called, "If Coach won't let you teach me here, maybe we can do some...*private* lessons? There's so much I want to *learn*."

Her innuendo was clear. Emory laughed.

"Sure thing, cutie," he called.

I saw red. Not metaphorically. Literally. My vision turned red while I imagined Emory covered in blood as I took his own damn skates to his neck.

The fantasy calmed me down...slightly.

"Lucy, you don't get to fuck around with my players. Period," I snapped.

This led to a bunch of chortling and muttering from my team about how they'd like Lucy to fuck around with them. Lucy just smiled, but I knew better, the way she played with her hair gave her away. It didn't matter that she'd done all this intentionally. If they embarrassed her, I'd kill them.

"Ms. Braverman, *now*. Don't make me wait," I said, voice low and steady and not fucking around one inch.

Glaring at me, she skated without difficulty to the edge of the rink, hopping gracefully off the ice and onto the insulated sub-floor.

"I'm here, your highness," she snapped. "At your bidding."

Oh, she had no idea what sort of bidding I actually wanted. An image of Lucy, naked, those nipples on full display and hard for me appeared in my mind. In it, she was kneeling, her hands tied behind her back with her panties, her mouth and throat full of my—

Bad man. I was a bad man.

"Stop mouthing off," I told her, swallowing down the rest of what I wanted to say, which was *or I'll give your mouth something better to do.*

Then I blew my whistle again.

"Team, Ms. Braverman is here with us for the rest of the season as my assistant. She'll be helping out by sweeping the ice, bringing you water, getting my dry cleaning...all sorts of fun activities, mainly because she keeps breaking the rules. And you all know how I feel about rulebreakers. Which means you all have a new rule. Any single one of you looks at her funny or touches her, even her hand, and you're out for the rest of the season. Think about her inappropriately and I'll know, and *you'll* be riding the bench."

"I'd rather ride the brat than the bench," Paul Westlake, who was my first line defenseman, muttered to Emory.

"Westlake, you're out for the rest of the season," I said, voice echoing off the boards and through the entire arena.

He gaped at me. "What the hell, Coach!"

"You heard me." I turned my head, making sure to look at every other member of my team. Including Emory and Mason, who were both smirking. "Anyone else have something to say?"

Silence.

Just the way I liked it.

Lucy was tugging on my sleeve, whispering, "Don't take your frustration with me out on them."

I ignored her.

"Okay, the rest of you are skating suicides for the rest of practice. I don't care if you puke, you'll keep going." To Lucy, I said, "And you'll be the one cleaning up the puke."

Her face turned green.

Under my breath, I said, "You want to fuck with me? I'll fuck with you right back."

She didn't need to know that the "with" felt optional.

♥ ♥

AFTER PRACTICE WAS OVER, I LEFT LUCY TO CLEAN UP THE three piles of vomit on the ice, satisfied that I'd taught her an appropriate lesson, and made my way to my office.

Trey followed me.

"Blake, this seems like a real mistake. Paul's one of our best players, and you benched him for the season for a dumb joke any of his teammates were probably thinking in their heads."

Trey was right, but I didn't want to hear it. It was the least I could've done in that moment, instead of ripping each and every limb off of Paul's body, including his dick. He'd embarrassed Lucy, even if no one knew but me. What's more, none of them were going to make a move on her now, which was exactly what I wanted.

"I'm setting an example," I told him as I entered my office.

To my annoyance, he followed me inside, grabbing the chair facing my desk, and turning it around so he could straddle it.

"Are you setting an example? Or are you pissing—inappropriately, I might add—all over your 'territory' like a college punk so the rest of these college punks stay away from her?" He put territory in quotes, and the accusation made my whole body go stiff, and not in the way it did when Lucy paraded around in one of her little outfits.

How much did he know?

"I'm not sure what you're talking about," I told Trey, sitting in my own chair and typing my password—Trouble-maker—so I could access my laptop and do work, ignoring the steaming pile of shit Trey was serving to me.

He raised an eyebrow. "I see it. I'm sure the players see it. The only ones who don't see it are Lucy—and you. It's a real problem, Coach. You can't have an affair or date a freshman at the university you work at, especially not when she's employed by the team."

"She's not really employed; she's doing her community service."

"Still. You're in a position of power over her. It looks really bad. She'll either have to drop out, or you'll have to quit. It would hurt you both—"

"Lucy's not dropping out," I barked. "She's going to vet school after college. It's her dream."

Trey stared at me. "Shit, this isn't just a case of being an old asshole who wants some young pussy. You have actual feelings for her, don't you?"

An image came to mind: Of me rising to my feet, grabbing Trey by the throat, and slamming him against the wall, and then again, and then again. No one talked about Lucy's pussy. No one talked about her like she was nothing more than *pussy*. I wanted to kill him for it.

Instead, I took a deep, long breath, reminding myself that attacking my assistant coach would be bad man behavior. As much as I wanted to, I needed to keep my shit together—now and forever.

I steepled my fingers. "Of course I have feelings *about* my legal ward," I lied easily, playing with semantics. "But if you're suggesting I'm romantically interested in her...well, your guess is as off as your aim was the last time we went golfing with the dean." I cleared my throat, hating what I was about to say next. "In fact, I was going to ask if you could give me your sister's number, so I could reach out to her about going on a date."

Trey frowned at me. "You already have her number."

Damn it. He was right. It had slipped my mind.

"You wouldn't be using her as a way to cover your own ass, would you?" he continued.

I straightened my shoulders. "Last I checked, I was your boss. So, I suggest you don't ask questions like that going forward, if you're interested in keeping your job. I must have not saved her number. Now, if you don't want to give it to me, that's fine, but I would like to take her out, so..."

God, I was a real asshole. Still, Trey swallowed, nodding and reciting his sister's number so I could put it in my phone. I had forgotten her name but figured that part didn't matter. I'd needed to get him off the scent, and I had. That was the important thing, even if I hated myself for it.

As he sat there, I shot off a quick text to his sister, letting her know who it was and asking if she wanted to get dinner. It was barely a minute before she responded with a *Yes!* The idea of going on a date with anyone made me feel sick to my stomach, and I had to remind myself that I wasn't in a relationship with Lucy. I wasn't in *anything* with Lucy, except for poorly misguided lust. Probably fucking someone else was the way to go.

Even though I knew my dick wouldn't get hard for anyone but her.

5

LUCY

"**L**ucy!"

I paused on the steps of the life sciences building, turning back to see Professor Alison Putrovksi clicking after me in her stilettos. The professor taught my animal biology class, and although she'd never entirely warmed to me, I always showed up to lectures, studied my ass off, and got perfect scores on all the exams. I knew people thought I was a ditzy blonde party girl, but as a kid who'd been ignored by everyone but the family dogs—only to lose both to cancer—I was determined to become a veterinarian.

It was one of the hardest educational paths: vet school admissions were even more competitive than med school. It was one of the reasons why I'd wanted to go to Reina originally; they had a much better pre-vet program. Instead, I was doing my best here at Tabb, and praying that my grades, extracurriculars, volunteering, internships, and recommendation letters would be enough.

I doubted working for the hockey team as an assistant

would do much, unless the admissions people were hockey fans.

"What did you need, professor?" I asked her when she reached me.

She seemed out of breath. "I have news—good news. Reina and Tabb are starting a joint pre-veterinary program, with shared courses and curriculum. The students who are accepted can be enrolled at either school, but they'll have to take summer classes. The competition will be fierce, of course: they're only accepting five students from all four years across both universities."

My heart started beating a little dance of excitement.

"That sounds tough," I said.

"Yes." She looked me up and down. "But I think you have what it takes to get in."

My heart did somersaults. I felt like I was going to throw up. "Really?"

"Really. Your grades and effort reflect that. All you need is to keep them up for the rest of the semester...and a hell of a recommendation letter. Which I'm willing to provide, as long as..." she hesitated.

"As long as what?" I prompted, my heart graduating to cartwheels.

"As long as you continue doing what you're doing," she finished, although it had seemed like she was about to say something else.

"I can make that happen," I promised. "Thank you so much. You have no idea..."

"Well, you're not in yet," the professor warned. "So don't thank me. But I have high hopes for you and your future, Lucy. Don't let me down."

"Of course."

I turned to go, and she put a hand on my shoulder.

"I was wondering..."

"Yes?"

"Coach Samson is your legal guardian, yes?"

Oh god, was I about to get in trouble for something else?

"Yes," I said. "He really doesn't have much to guard now that I'm eighteen. Although you try telling him that."

She blinked.

Whoops.

"He's overprotective," I explained.

"Oh," she smiled. "That's an excellent trait in a father figure."

Trepidation filled my lungs. Where was she going with this?

"Do you...happen to know if he's single?"

It was my turn to blink. My breath caught in my chest.

"He...is. Why?"

Although I already knew why. Blake was hot, wealthy from his pro days and from the hefty salary Tabb paid him, responsible...a real catch.

"My brother is his assistant coach, and I've met him a few times. He set us up, but I want to make sure I'm not wasting my time barking up the wrong tree."

She laughed. It was a nervous laugh, and had it been in relation to any other man, I would've felt sympathy for her. As it was, all I felt was rage and hurt. Coach was going on a date with *her*? *She* was going on a date with Coach? I'd never known him to go on dates, even though deep down I knew he must be having sex with *someone*. But to be confronted with it, and for it to be my professor...what was he playing at?

"No," I forced myself to say. Because why did I care? I wasn't supposed to care. Not anymore. "No, he's not dating anyone as far I know. We don't really talk about that stuff, though."

Relief spread across her face in a sweet smile. "Alright, thank you. Of course, since he's your guardian and I'm your professor, I know that this is...a little awkward. You're okay with it, aren't you?"

No.

Absolutely the fuck not.

Stay away from him, bitch.

But I couldn't say any of that, so instead I smiled back at her.

"I have no reason not to be. Have fun on your date!" I glanced down at my phone. "Oh damn, I have to go to a study session at the library, but thank you so much again for the information about the program, professor. I'm really grateful."

"Of course, Lucy." She squeezed my shoulder. "You're a good kid and deserve the best of everything. And who knows, maybe we'll be celebrating together one day!"

Because she saw herself as "part of the family."

I kept the fake smile on my face as I walked away, only dropping it when there was no one in sight.

It was time to get over Coach Blake Samson.

And I was going to have to do it by getting under someone else.

6

BLAKE

I'd lost my fucking mind.

I needed to call a psychiatrist. Or head straight to the police station and turn myself in.

Because I was currently in Lucy's dorm room. It was prime class time, and no one was in the building, giving me enough cover for what I'd come here to do.

And what I'd come to do was install cameras and mics everywhere.

I was keeping an eye on her. I was worried about what she'd do next. I was trying to protect her, since she refused to protect herself.

That's what I was telling myself, anyway. Too bad it was all goddamn lies.

The truth was watching her flirt with my players, flipping her hair, pressing her breasts into their chests and joking with them was driving me up the fucking wall. What was worse was seeing the way their eyes followed her *everywhere*. Someone might as well have been ripping my nails off my fingers, one by one, and no amount of making them do bag skates felt like proper punishment.

Watching her flirt with Emory and suggest *private lessons* when everyone in the vicinity knew she didn't mean skating ...dread had filled my stomach. I didn't know if Lucy was a virgin, but I did know that if she ever let that punk's dick near her, I'd kill him.

Thus, I found myself in her dorm room, hiding cameras and mics where she wouldn't see them. I'd gotten them from a man named Micah Feldman, who was the older brother of Jack, the captain of our rival hockey team. Micah had smirked when I'd refused to tell him why I needed the cameras.

"There's always that one woman that makes us lose all sense of control, isn't there?" He'd laughed and then shown me how to install a GPS tracker on her phone, which I'd done when she'd left her purse alone at practice one day.

I had a problem. I'd always kept a tight tether on my worst impulses. There was a darkness in me, a violence that I'd been hiding since I was an orphaned foster kid lost in the system and fighting to protect my foster siblings, only for no one to protect me. And then the fighting stopped being about protecting others and became a way to express my anger at a world that refused to protect me. That was until Lucy's father showed up in my life as my Big Brother in that after-school program and introduced me to hockey and a better future.

Since then, keeping myself leashed hadn't been an issue...until months ago, when a curvy little dynamo sashayed her way back into my life and sent my control haywire. That leash was fraying, and I was pretty sure it was going to snap soon if I didn't do anything about it.

Maybe I should've just let Lucy get expelled. Then she'd be far, far away. Except everything in me rejected the idea of letting her out of my sight.

Just as I placed the last camera in the tiny sliver of an opening between her mirror and the frame that faced her bed, I heard a sultry laugh. It echoed in my ears, a siren's song...and a warning.

Fuck.

As the knob turned, I scanned the room. The closet was much too small for my big frame, there was no bathroom, I wasn't about to shimmy out the tiny window and plunge four stories to the ground. My only option was either for my ward to catch me in her room, or to—

—hide under the bed like the creep I was.

It took some maneuvering, but I managed to slide underneath, holding my breath as the door opened.

She was still laughing as she entered the tiny room, and the sound wrapped around my body, rubbing over the hair on my chest, the nerve endings on the back of my neck. A laugh shouldn't have made me hard, but the sound shot right to my balls.

Fuck me.

Her laughter died down as she slipped out of her flip flops. Goddamn it, we'd talked about those flip flops. It was a stupid thing, but Lucy had flat feet, and flip flops were terrible for arch support and posture. Not to mention, she drove with them on, and I always worried she was going to get the thong of the flip flop caught on the brake and get in a horrible accident. But whenever I told her to wear some real shoes, she laughed at me, called me an uptight ass, and bought more flip flops.

What was she doing back from class so early? I had her schedule memorized; she should be in a study session right now.

There was the snick of the belt, the whisper of a zipper, and then tiny jean shorts joined her flip flops on the floor, followed by a green tank top...and a black lace bralette.

Fuck me ten ways to hell and back.

Well, maybe she'd come back to change and then she'd head out and I could get out of here. I could smell her, something fruity and floral I couldn't place. She smelled like sunshine, she smelled like sex, she smelled like everything I'd ever wanted and could never have.

Because she's eighteen, Blake. And you're her legal guardian.

What would her parents have said?

Except that it had become clear early on that Lucy's parents hadn't cared much about what happened to her. Her father might have looked out for me, but that hadn't translated to his daughter. I wasn't sure who really had looked out for her, and when I thought about it, really thought about it, I was plagued with guilt for sending her away for so long.

Guess I'm on my own again, she'd said in the note she written me before she'd left for boarding school. I still had that note in my desk drawer at home. I didn't know why I'd kept it. Maybe it was meant to be a reminder of all the ways I'd failed her...failed, period.

My dark thoughts were interrupted by Lucy's bare feet, tiny and cute with Barbie Pink polish. There was a creak and the bed sagged underneath her body.

Ah, shit. Don't tell me she was taking a nap. How the hell was I getting out of here?

Although it quickly became apparent it was worse. With a small sigh, she murmured to herself, "God, I'm so horny," and despite knowing what I was doing was wrong, I strained my ears to hear what came next.

Shallow breaths and sighs, some shifting as she got into position. I didn't have to see her to imagine what she was doing. Stroking a hand over her neck, making her way down to her bare breasts, a small gasp as she tweaked her nipples. Did she like it gentle, or rough? Did she want it to hurt? What color were her nipples? Her breasts were large and perky, I knew that from the tight little tank tops and crop tops she wore that left little to the imagination.

Then a moan. Was her hand sneaking its way down between those round, thick thighs? Was she stroking herself? Fast or slow?

"God, I'm so wet," she whimpered.

She was.

I could hear it.

I could fucking *smell* it.

If I'd thought she'd smelled like sex before...a sweet musk scented the air, and my nostrils flared in response. I licked my lips like I could taste it, taste *her*. And even though it was so very wrong, I shoved my hand under my pants, not daring to unzip in case she could hear it, and grabbed my hard cock.

I was going to hell, but I couldn't help myself. That tether was about to snap.

Each slick sound of her stroking herself, every gasp and moan and sigh was just one more thread losing its grip and giving up the cause. I squeezed my cock in tempo with Lucy, staring up at the bed frame like I had x-ray vision and could see her. There was the brush of wet fabric. Did she leave her panties on when she touched herself? Why? Was there a little bit of shyness there, resistance, embarrassment that kept her from touching herself directly? That wouldn't do. If I were with her, I'd make her take those panties off, make her look me in the eye as she touched her clit and explored her little hole in front of me, make those gasps turn into cries before I shoved my head between her legs and...

Fuck.

My hand squeezed my cock tighter.

I was the worst man in existence. But I couldn't stop myself, especially as the wet sound of silk rubbing against soaked skin sped up. So did her moans and gasps, and the bed shifted as she...god, was she humping the air?

What was she thinking about? *Who* was she thinking about? If it was Emory, there'd be nothing left when I was done with him.

God, I was so fucked in the head.

I pulled my hand away from my cock. I needed to interrupt her, needed to get the fuck out of from under her bed, go directly to the police precinct and ask them to lock me up for life—

"Coooooooach," she whimpered.

No, fuck no.

And then, "Blaaaaaake, please, daddy, please—"

As she cried out my name, cried out *daddy*, in the sweetest sound I'd ever heard, high-pitched, breathless, and *needy*, I came.

In my pants.

Like a motherfucking teenager.

There was a thud as she fell back on the bed.

"Stupid, stupid, stupid," she was muttering to herself, sounding pissed. "This is the last time I get off to thoughts of him. I'm *done*."

There was a sniffle.

Was she crying?

Even though I'd managed to stay under the bed for that whole magnificent ordeal, the thought of her crying—over *me*—made it almost impossible not to get out from underneath this bed, sweep her up in my arms, and comfort her in my lap.

Why was she so upset?

"I hate you, Blake Samson," she groaned. "I hate how much I want you. And I hate myself for this, most. You're an idiot, Lucy Braverman."

And then she was hopping off the bed, wriggling her legs. Her panties, also hot pink and lacy, dropped to the carpeted floor, inches away from me, as her feet padded to her closet. I held my breath, watching her slip shower slides onto her feet, wrap a towel around her body, and walk to the door. It opened and shut, leaving me alone, heart pounding, pants wet with my own cum.

The tether had snapped.

I'd lost complete control.

And I needed to get the hell out of here and get my head on straight. I wasn't sure what that would take, but god, I would do whatever it took to regain control over myself.

Sliding out from under the bed, I rose, lightheaded from all the blood that had gone to my cock and left my brain, surveying her room, the rumpled bed, the cameras focused on her. I'd be able to watch the video of her coming, relive the moments of my greatest shame and greatest joy.

"Blake, you fool," I muttered to myself, only half aware I was echoing Lucy's own frustration with herself. But that neediness in her voice, the possibility that what she needed was me, and I was the only one who could provide and fulfill them for her...

Before I could think better of it, I was lifting her wet panties to my nose like I could inhale that imaginary emotional bond, smelling her, sweet musk, sex, and sunshine, then pressing the wet gusset to my lips and tongue, trying to suck out whatever juices and taste of her again.

Like a goddamn teenager, my cock got hard again. I hadn't had a refractory period like this in years.

Slipping her wet panties into my pocket, I shoved away the implications of my actions—all of them—and slipped out the door before she could catch me and I'd have to confront her and what I'd done.

This is a one-time thing. You'll get your shit back together, I told myself.

It was a goddamn lie.

Someone had stolen my panties.

I stood in my small, pink and black decorated dorm room, in my pink robe, hair up in a towel, staring down at the floor. I'd dropped them after my "personal playtime." I knew it for a fact. So how were they not there? Was I losing my mind?

And what the hell was that smell in my room? It smelled like...well, a little like me when I came, but harsher, darker, deeper, thicker.

Did I need to go to health services to find out if I had a yeast infection?

Still in my robe, I crawled on the floor, looking under the bed. Not there. I checked the laundry hamper too, and the bed, in case I was losing my mind, but deep down, I knew I wasn't.

Which meant some asshole, some *creeper*, had been in my room and stolen my recently-orgasmed-in panties while I'd been showering.

Who? Was someone in my hall fucking with me? Did I have a stalker? Was it one of the hockey players I'd been flirting with? My TA had canceled the study session today, so I'd come back early. Angry, hurt, and needing to self-soothe, I'd taken care of myself, even though I'd hated myself for it. Hated that I'd tried to fantasize about someone, anyone else, and failed. Hated that even though I was surrounded by attractive guys all the time, the one man I couldn't have, shouldn't have, would never look at me like I was more than an annoying and immature child, was the only image I could get myself off to. And when I'd come, it had felt like there was someone in the room with me, watching, listening...

I shook that off. Someone was fucking with me, for sure, and I was going to go to hockey practice this evening like I always did, and I was going to find out if one of those sweaty, stinky assholes was behind it.

♥‚♥

When I got to practice, Coach wasn't even there. I tried to ignore the stomach drop of disappointment of not seeing him, telling myself it was better that I didn't. Anyone else, I could have handled it. But with Blake, I knew I wouldn't be able to hide my embarrassment after getting myself off to thoughts of him fucking me.

I skidded up to Emory on the ice where he was running drills with Mason.

"What are you doing out here, babe?" he asked, raising an eyebrow.

I rolled my eyes. The babe was for show. Emory wasn't into me. He had the hots for some older woman far out of his league, and even though he refused to tell any of us who it was, I had my guesses. But that didn't mean he and his friends hadn't decided to scare me or embarrass me.

"Did you take my panties?" I asked him point blank.

He skidded to a stop on the ice, dropping his stick and backing away from me.

"What the actual fuck?"

"Did you take my panties?" I enunciated, angry but also hopeful it was a prank and not something worse.

But based on the shock and confusion on his face, my gut told me otherwise. Dread pooled in my stomach.

"Just tell me the truth," I asked. "Because my panties disappeared from my room while I was in the shower..."

Mason looked concerned. "Are you sure?"

"Positive."

Emory shook his head. "Wasn't me. I was...well I was busy all morning, and I wouldn't know how to break into your room anyway. But maybe it was one of these other horny assholes."

Lifting his hands to his face, he yelled, "Hey, you motherfuckers, stop what you're doing and get over here!"

Oh no.

Oh no, oh no, oh no.

This could get messy.

"Emory," I warned. "Please don't."

The whole team stopped practicing, skating over.

"What's up?" Matt, Emory's roommate asked.

"Did any of you go to Lucy's room and steal her panties today?"

A loud, manly chorus of shocked "no" and "what the actual fuck, who would do that shit" echoed through the arena. Players circled me, eyeing me up and down, and even though a few of them smirked, most of them seemed worried.

"We wouldn't do shit like that, but I tell you what, if we find out who did—" one began.

A whistle blew, interrupting us.

I looked up, directly into my legal guardian's eyes as he stared back. He looked pissed, although for once, not at me.

"What are you idiots doing? Why isn't anyone practicing? Why are you all circling our team assistant like you're about to tear her apart?"

Was that...did he sound protective?

I gaped at him.

"Nah, Coach. We're trying to be helpful. Some creepy fuckwad stole Lucy's panties out of her dorm room and she thought it was one of us."

Oh.

My.

God.

I didn't have to look in a mirror to know my face had gone bright red. Any ability to keep myself regulated and hide my embarrassment had flown out the window as soon as Blake had arrived. And being blonde and fair skinned, there was no way in hell I could hide a blush. My whole body felt like it was on fire. This was my nightmare, talking about my panties in front of the man whose face I had imagined when I'd made them wet...

There was a dark, unreadable look in his eyes. Usually I could tell what he was thinking, but right now the look was masked. Probably because he had no interest in hearing anything about my panties.

"That's sick," he said, slipping a hand into his pocket. He shut his eyes for a moment, and then when he opened them, he said, "I'm sorry, Lucy. We'll take care of this." Then, all business, he blew his whistle again.

"But that's it. I'll take care of it. The rest of you, get back to drills. Lucy, get off the ice before you slip and fall and we have to sue the university or file worker's comp."

I straightened.

Well.

If he could dismiss something so scary so easily, then he hadn't seemed protective at all. No, this was annoyance. If Coach had his way, he'd never have met me. I swallowed down frustrated tears, not even wanting to think about how much it sucked that he didn't really give a shit about me beyond being his responsibility.

So, I flipped my hair. "I think I'll stay on the ice," I said sweetly. "I can help the team better from here."

"She's our good luck charm, aren't you, cutie," one of the other players said, winking at me.

God, why did it do nothing for me? Why was the only person who made me feel a frisson of excitement glaring at me like I was the unwanted stray puppy who'd pissed his bed?

"Lucy, if you don't get off the ice, I'll haul you off myself," Blake warned.

I grinned at him, twirling my hair. "You sure you can carry me? I'm pretty thick and you're getting old."

Players hooted, except for Mason, who raised an eyebrow, watching me.

What the hell are you doing? he mouthed.

I couldn't answer him because I had no idea. I was playing with fire and was going to get scorched, but I was so hurt, angry, and scared, I welcomed the burn.

Coach threw back his head and laughed. And, completely shocking me, he pushed open the door to the ice and walked out on it in his suit and dress shoes, making his way across without slipping once. The players parted for him like he was Moses and they were the Red Sea, and then he was bending down and I was being lifted and thrown over his shoulder like a sack of potatoes.

I smacked his back.

"Blake, what the hell are you doing? Put me down! You're embarrassing me!"

He was. But worse, he was turning me back on. He'd never gotten this close to me since my parents' funeral, and being carried by him, surrounded by his peat and honey smell, was exciting and comforting in a way that I couldn't stand. My nose was pressed up against his back, and if I wanted to, I could lick his suit jacket.

Instead, I bit him.

"Stop," he muttered, ignoring the team's whispers as he gripped my thigh in warning. He was stabilizing me and threatening me, I knew that, but his hand was so close to my pussy I wondered if he could feel the heat radiating from it.

Would he notice?

Would he care?

"I can't believe you're doing this," I grumbled.

"You gave me no goddamn choice," he said, and then we were back past the boards and in the bleachers and he was lowering me to the padded floor. He didn't release me though, his hands sliding up and gripping my waist with one hand, my shoulder with the other. I looked up at him, and suddenly everyone else disappeared, until it was only the two of us. I hadn't been this close to him in so long and his green eyes were as mysterious and breathtaking as an enchanted forest...same as they'd always been.

"What—" I said.

"Lucy, I've warned you in the past. Don't push me," he said.

"And what will you do if I keep pushing?" My voice was

breathy. If I stepped even a centimeter forward, my hard nipples would brush the fabric covering his chest.

His eyes, before so secretly expressive, shuttered, and he released me, taking a step back.

"You don't want to know, I promise you that," he said. "Now, get out of my sight. You've caused enough trouble for the day."

I blinked.

God, his moods were so mercurial. I didn't know what he was reacting to, but I knew it *hurt*.

I was done with this man.

So done.

"Whatever," I said. "Clearly someone is stalking me and stealing my panties and you don't even care. What kind of guardian are you, if you don't guard?"

He snorted. "Lucy, no one is stalking you. I promise. Someone is probably playing a prank, or you're just being forgetful. You've lost ten iPhones in your life—I know because I had to pay for all the replacements—I'm not surprised you misplaced a pair of your underwear. But now you're making it my team's problem, which means you're making it my problem. I don't have time for this shit, so I need you to go."

I don't have time for this shit.

As in, I don't have time for you.

So, so done.

Unable to look him in the eyes anymore, knowing that I might actually lose control of the tears that threatened to spill out at his dismissive rejection, I looked down. One of his pockets looked wrinkled and a little bulgy, and even though I wanted to fix it for him, fuss over him, I knew better. He'd never let me touch him. This was the only time, and...

...Time to move on. I'd said I had already, but I meant it. For real this time.

"I'm going," I told him. "Don't expect me to come back."

But instead of reacting, he stared forward, ignoring me as I forced myself to flip my hair and sway my hips as I headed out of the arena, and hopefully, out of his life.

He didn't look at me once.

Time to do something drastic. No more getting off to him or fantasizing about him or pushing him or flirting with him. Not when he had a date soon. Not when he cared so little about my safety, about me.

Yup, getting under someone for the first time was the way to go.

8

BLAKE

M y hands were gripping my home office chair so
hard, my knuckles had gone white. My breath
was so hot, smoke might as well have been
leaking from my mouth.

I watched the cameras. Lucy paced her small room as
she said on speaker phone with her friend Leslie, "...which
is why I need to lose my virginity. Tonight."

"Are you sure this is a good idea? Maybe you're being a
little too reactive."

"He couldn't have given a shit. He dismissed my
concerns, made it seem like I was overreacting—I felt like a
kicked puppy, and I refuse to feel that way."

Pain, sharp and angry, shot through my chest. I had been
so embarrassed and disgusted with myself for being the
stalker she'd been worried about, I'd been cold to her. Cruel.
Her panties had been in my pocket the whole time as I lied
to her and gaslit her.

What Lucy needed was care and acceptance. She was
about to go make a reckless choice, one that every bone in

my body loathed, and it was because of me. I'd done it to her.

"If Blake Samson doesn't want me, I'll find someone who will."

My chair arm cracked in half from the force of my hand gripping it tight.

I did want her. Badly. So badly, I was about to make the worst decision of my life. But I would die before I let another man touch her, feel her, thrust inside that untried pussy and took what shouldn't be mine but I was going to make mine anyway.

"So, what's the plan?" Leslie asked.

"There's a ritzy hotel in town. The Ramore. I'm going to get dressed up and go sit in the bar and wait for a man—not a boy—to approach me. If he's cute enough," she shrugged, her oversized sweater falling off her shoulder so I could see her perfect, bare, innocent, *virginal* skin. "Then I'll fuck him."

"What if they think you're a sex worker?"

Lucy laughed. "So what? That's a completely respectable job. And I'd happily take someone's money."

Leslie must have digested that, because then she asked, "And what if no one's cute enough?"

"Someone will have to be..."

"Emory..." Leslie trailed off.

"Is obsessed with his mystery woman. He doesn't want me. Besides, a boy isn't going to get me over this. I need a man."

"Well," Leslie said brightly. "I'm excited to celebrate the loss of your virginity with you tomorrow. Breakfast at the dorm cafeteria?"

Lucy snorted, and as she looked in the mirror, I could

see her reflection. Even as she blew herself a kiss, she didn't look excited or even nervous.

Just...sad.

"You're paying, though," Lucy said.

Before I could stop myself, I was out of my broken chair, ready to run down the stairs, grab my keys, and head out the door. I glanced quickly at the photos lined up in the office, each of Lucy at different ages, with frizzy hair, without frizzy hair, with braces, grinning, looking sad and determined... the last was of Lucy in her graduation cap and gown, a graduation I had missed.

I froze.

I couldn't do this. I shouldn't do this.

She wasn't a kid anymore. I couldn't ignore that fact, not when I'd heard her come today, not when her panties still lay folded in my pocket, not when her body had practically brushed against my chest.

If Lucy wanted to lose her virginity...

...well, I couldn't let that happen.

Unless it's you, that dark voice in my head supplied.

No. I wouldn't fuck her.

But I wouldn't let her fuck anyone else, either.

9

LUCY

L eslie had been right.

They *did* think I was a sex worker.

More than ten men—all older, some much, much, much older—had hit on me tonight, buying me drinks and propositioning me.

"How much?" one had asked, and even though he'd been attractive and smelled good, I told him with a smile I was waiting for someone and watched him shrug and walk away.

I didn't want anyone. I wasn't turned on *at all*. All I wanted to do was go home and get in bed and cry over the fact that the one man I wanted didn't want me. Was maybe even on a date with someone else. Someone age-appropriate who held my future in her hands.

Currently, I was in the women's bathroom, staring at myself in the mirror. A sad but determined girl looked back. It was a look I recognized, one I'd seen in the mirror many times, when my parents rejected me, when I had milestones but no one to share them with. Until I'd met Leslie, I'd never even really had a real friend, just boys who wanted to sleep with me and girls who wanted to keep me close so I didn't sleep with their boyfriends...as if I would.

"You can do this, Braverman," I told my reflection. "You *need* to do this. What, are you going to be, an eighty-year-old virgin because of a stupid childhood crush?"

I heard laughter. In the mirror, a woman stood behind me, watching. She grinned.

"Honey, I've been in your position. And I promise you, the only way to get over someone..."

Yeah, yeah.

"Is to get under someone else. I know," I said.

"Good." She wielded her lipstick at me like a baton. "Now, you go get yourself under someone."

"Will do."

I squared my shoulders, fixed my lipstick, and with one confident wink I didn't feel, turned and headed back out to the lobby bar.

The bartender, a cute dude with glasses, nodded at me when I hopped back on the barstool I'd been sitting in earlier.

"Kept it safe for you," he said. "Kept your drink safe for you, too."

I blinked. "My drink?"

He tilted his head. "Gentleman on the other side of the bar bought it for you. Said you seemed like a French 75 kind of woman."

I had no idea if I was a French 75 kind of woman. I didn't even know what a French 75 was. I was a freshman in college; my drink of choice was tequila shots with too much salt and lime.

Still, I'd try it.

Searching out the man who'd gotten it for me, my eyes widened.

Because he was *hot.*

Tall, broad, blond, in a clearly bespoke suit and tie, he stared back at me with green, mischievous eyes and an easy smile. They were a paler green than Coach's eyes, thank god.

Tipping the drink at the hot man, I took a sip.

It was way too sweet, and I tried not to make a face but failed.

I saw him laugh.

Then he rose from his seat and made his way over to me.

I waited, putting the drink down. I didn't care that he'd bought it for me, there was no way I was drinking that.

"Not a French 75 woman, I take it?" the man inquired when he reached me.

"I guess not," I said. "Honestly, I like tequila shots."

He raised an eyebrow. "Well, I haven't had a tequila shot in ten years, but there's a first and last time for everything, I guess."

I giggled. "Then let's do shots."

The bartender shook his head but pulled out a top-shelf tequila and poured two shots.

"I need training wheels," I admitted, and he added a slice of lime and held out a saltshaker.

"I'll take this," the man standing next to me said, and grabbing the salt, held it out. "Want to give me your hand?" he asked, and I handed it to him. Bending down, he placed a kiss on the skin between my thumb and forefinger. The tiniest of tingles ran through me.

This one.

I was barely into him, but barely would have to be enough tonight.

Then he licked my hand and poured some salt on it.

I felt nothing.

"Ready?" he asked.

I wasn't.

I really wasn't.

But what choice did I have? It was either this—shots and sex—or go home and mope until I got old. I was a lot of things, but pathetic wasn't one of them.

Although, isn't it pathetic to lose your virginity to someone who you're barely into just to avoid your feelings about someone else?

I ignored the bitch in my head and her honest question. I didn't need that right now.

Lifting the shot glass with my other hand, I clinked it with the nameless man, looking into his eyes as I licked up the salt, poured the drink down my throat.

Fire burned through me, heating my insides and calming me down.

Yup, I could do this.

"So, what's a beautiful woman like you doing at a place like this?" he asked.

I rolled my eyes, sucking on the lime, delighting in the way his eyes heated. "Does that line usually work for you?"

He moved in closer, running his free hand over my bare shoulder. I was in a red dress that was tight enough to be a second skin. It showed *everything*. I'd even been tempted to take a photo of myself and send it to Coach, but his perfunctory fatherly bullshit, or more likely, silence, would've hurt even more.

The man appreciated my dress; it was clear by the way his eyes roved over my body.

"Well?" he prompted.

I figured honesty wouldn't hurt. "Trying to distract myself from silly heartbreak," I said.

That made him cough. "What kind of man would be stupid enough to break your heart?"

I shrugged.

"An idiot. A fool," he decided. "Complete moron to let you slip through his fingers. Lucky for me though, because I'm happy to pick up where he left off." He held out his hand. "My name's Sam."

Something prompted me to say, "Lacy."

Why, I didn't know, but giving him my real name felt way too...personal.

What's more personal than letting him stick his dick in your vagina? that voice asked.

Shut up, I thought back.

And, doing my best to shut her up, I looked at him from under my lashes. "And where exactly would you pick up, Sam?"

"Well, if I can be this forward: I'd bring you up to my hotel room and do my best to make you come enough times to forget him."

My eyes widened.

"That *is* forward."

He chuckled. "I'm not sure if there's any reason for us to waste time, Lacy."

Then he was bending forward, wrapping his hand around my hair, and pulling me in to kiss me.

I felt nothing. Well, a hint of something, but compared to the way I'd felt this afternoon when Coach had thrown me over his shoulder...

The kiss turned open mouthed, urgent—on his side— and I closed my eyes and let myself fall into it. With my eyes closed, I could pretend he was someone else, and that helped.

Pulling back, he whistled.

"Yeah, that other man is a moron. What do you say?"

No.

I don't want to go upstairs with you.

I could feel the thought in my very skin.

But I could also remember the derision in Coach's eyes from earlier, and that settled that.

Instead of answering, I slid off the barstool and placed my hand in his.

"I say yes," I told him, ignoring the way my body rejected each and every word.

"Lacy…" The bartender coughed, his eyes focused on something behind me.

"What?" I asked.

He shook his head. "Nothing."

As Sam led me through the bar and into the hotel lobby, I swore I felt someone staring at me, burning my bare back with their gaze. But when I turned to look, no one was watching.

10

BLAKE

I wasn't going to pretend I wasn't a violent man. My whole need for control stemmed from that deep-seated brutality within me. I'd been in fights with foster fathers, with classmates, and players from opposing teams. I knew I had a vicious soul. But I'd never realized just how vicious it was until I sat in a booth at the Ramore Hotel bar, nursing a whiskey, watching Lucy do tequila shots with some douchebag finance bro who was much too old for her.

I was in a shadowed corner where she wouldn't notice me, making it easy to stew in my possessive rage as she flirted with the blond asshole. Even knowing *I'd* pushed her to do this, that this was *my* fault, didn't lessen the need to punish her for her reckless behavior. I balled my free hand into a fist as if that would keep me from storming across the bar and punching that fucking asshole in the face. And then I'd shove Lucy over the bar, deliver swat after swat to her ass until it was glowing red and she and every other jackass in the place knew she was mine, right before I fucked that virgin pussy and claimed her for good...

The bartender currently serving Lucy and the douchebag flirting with her glanced up and caught my eyes. His went wide—very wide. I couldn't see myself, but I must have looked scary enough to disturb him, so I turned back to my drink, trying to pretend I was lost in thought instead of staring at the beautiful vixen as she sucked on a lime and every man's head swiveled to watch her do it. I palmed the top of the glass like I wanted to palm my dick. The thing was, Lucy wasn't unaware of her beauty. She knew she was beautiful. She liked it. She used it. It didn't turn me off, if anything, it made me respect her more for it. Her confidence made my cock hard, and even though I wanted to blind every other man in that bar, I didn't blame her for embracing her sexuality head on.

Plucking out all those other jackasses' eyeballs sounded like a good time, though.

Lucy said something to the man, and whatever he said in response made her jaw drop. She shook her head, her hair flying everywhere—hair I wanted to see spread across *my* pillow, not whipping some asshole in the face. I gripped the top of the glass tight in my hand. Could I convince her to wear a wig?

And then all thoughts of wigs disappeared as when that motherfucking cocky asshole, who must have had a death wish even if he didn't realize it yet, grabbed Lucy's hair and tugged her head back.

And fucking *kissed* her.

Kissed Lucy.

My Lucy.

Mine.

There was the slam of glass on solid wood, the tinkling sound of something breaking, and then sharp, burning pain shot through my hand. Curious as to why, I glanced down, only to see crushed shards everywhere. In my anger, I'd slammed my whiskey down hard on the table while squeezing the top, and the force must have cracked the lip, cutting my hand in the process.

This motherfucking bar. Not only did they make it easy for douchebags to prey on women, they also didn't even make their fucking drinkware strong enough to withstand some physical pressure.

As I rose to go give the fucking bartender a piece of my mind—and drag Lucy the fuck out of here in the process, and maybe use a broken shard to stab the man she was with—she slid off the barstool.

And then put her goddamn hand in his.

And led him out the bar.

Oh, absolutely the fuck not.

I must have thrown my drink, because I heard a shout and then more glass shattering. Rising from the booth, blood trickling down my hand, I approached the bartender. He was still watching me, shaking his head.

"I should throw you out of the bar," he told me.

"Do you know what that fucker said to her before they left?" I demanded, ignoring his half-assed threat.

He raised an eyebrow at me. "Why? Angry to see your daughter out and about?"

"She's not my fucking daughter," I told him.

He nodded. "I figured. Fathers usually don't react that way." Pointing at my hand, he asked, "Need me to clean that up for you?"

I shook my head. "I keep a first aid kit in my car."

It had come in handy various times in my life, including when Lucy had scraped up her knee as a kid, but I'd never expected to have to use it in a situation like this.

"Do you know what he said to her?" I asked again.

"I'm sure you can guess, man," the bartender said. "Look—"

I didn't wait to hear the rest as I headed out of the bar and the hotel to the parking lot. I assumed the combination of cool, fresh air and dark night would have calmed me down some.

It did the opposite. As I walked through the lobby, I noted which floor the elevator had stopped on: nine. That must be where Lucy was.

Every step I took toward my car was a step further away from Lucy. Every breath I took was an opportunity for him to touch her. I unlocked my car, ripping open the glove compartment so hard, the handle came off. Tossing it onto the seat, I pulled out my first aid kit before striding back into the hotel toward a bathroom.

"Sir," someone called, likely alarmed that I was leaving a trail of blood in my wake. I ignored them, storming toward the men's bathroom and heading inside, where I quickly cleaned and bandaged the cut, tossed the bloody paper towel I'd used to clean myself up in the trash and walked to the elevator, jamming my finger impatiently on the up button. Every second that ticked by was another second that man could be touching what was mine, tasting what was mine, fucking what was mine—

If I'd had another glass, I'd have smashed that one, too.

Finally, the elevator arrived, and I stepped inside. An older couple joined me, watching me warily as if I was someone dangerous. They were right. I was someone dangerous, just not to them.

But that finance douchebag better hope he hadn't touched her, and he better also hope he could run fucking fast.

Because if he had touched her and he couldn't run at the speed of light?

I was going to motherfucking kill him.

11

LUCY

I regretted my decision the second Sam followed me into his room and closed the door. The room was large, beautiful, elaborate in a Louis XV sort of way, and I hated everything about it. It reminded me of my parents' house. When I was young, I hadn't been allowed to sit on any of the surfaces except for a "child's couch," in case I got sweaty or sticky stains on any of the expensive furniture. That thought swept away any anticipation I had over finally having sex.

Sam watched me. "You know, Lacy, you don't have to do this."

I shook my head, smiling and approaching him. "I want to."

Reaching up, I pulled his head down to mine, kissing him open mouthed and eager, because I was going to act like I wanted him until I actually did. With a groan, he kissed me back, pushing me toward the bed as he slid the straps of my dress over my shoulders and tugged it down my body.

Pausing, he looked at my breasts in the red lace bra and shook his head.

"Gorgeous," he murmured. Bending down, he kissed my neck.

Nothing.

My clavicle.

Still nothing.

Making his way down to my breasts, I steeled myself for feeling more of nothing. Boys had done similar things to me before. I'd even let one get to second base in the past, and I had a feeling this was going to suck as much as that had. Also, I was worried the sex itself was going to hurt. Fortunately, I always came prepared. I had lube and condoms, and hopefully the combo would—

The door burst open with a loud crack and bang. And then Sam was being dragged away from me. Someone threw him across the room. He slammed into the wall and fell with a thud.

My eyes went wide.

Was I dreaming?

Because Blake stood in front of me, chest heaving, all hulked out with his veins popping and right hand wrapped in gauze, his green eyes burning with rage.

"I'll deal with you in a moment, troublemaker," he promised me, then turned and stalked over to Sam groaning on the floor.

At least he was alive.

Pulling up the straps of my dress to cover myself, I rushed forward to protect him.

"Blake, what the hell are you doing?" I screamed, trying to block him.

He didn't seem to care. Like I weighed no more than a feather, he lifted me with his unbandaged hand and deposited me behind him before he bent down and placed a shoe on Sam's neck.

"You touch her?" he growled.

Sam gasped.

"Tell me." Blake removed his foot. "Did. You. Touch. Her?"

"Blake, stop." I tried to drag him away by his arm, but I was no match for his strength—or anger.

"Yes, but I didn't know she was with someone."

"She's a kid."

"No, I'm not," I said indignantly, forgetting the situation we were in for a moment. "I'm eighteen, you asshole."

"What, you her dad or something?" Sam spat, face mottled.

Blake replaced his foot on his neck. "Nowhere near it. But she's *mine*, and I'm this close to killing you."

Mine.

Mine.

Mine.

The word echoed in my head like a gunshot pinging around a fun house.

What did he mean by mine? And god, why did it make me feel so good? The complete nothing I'd felt earlier was replaced with butterflies.

"I swear to god, I will call the cops," I said.

"Did he hurt you?" Blake asked.

"No."

"Fine." He removed his foot from Sam's throat. "Get the fuck out of here, and if you ever come near her again, I *will* kill you. Mark my words. Oh, and don't you fucking dare call the police or send security up here. The room is ours for the night."

Sam took him for his word, because he scuttled backward, stood on shaky legs, and without a look at me, ran out of the open door.

Leaving me alone with a version of my guardian I'd never seen before.

Part of me was still stuck on *mine* and all its implications as it swelled through my chest and gave me foolish hope.

But Blake was probably just feeling stupidly *fatherly*.

What are you, her dad or something?

Nowhere near it.

The other part of me was livid. How dare he follow me here and interrupt my sex plans?!

Blake turned to me. "Now it's your turn. What the fuck were you thinking?"

Oh, no.

No.

"What the hell were you doing? You could've killed him! And what did you do to your hand?"

I expected regret to flash in Blake's eyes, but there was nothing. He didn't even bother to answer my questions as he advanced on me.

"He deserved worse," Blake said.

"For what? Seducing a willing, *of age* partner? You don't own me, Blake Samson. I'm eighteen now, you aren't even really my guardian anymore."

There. I'd said it. Finally.

This time, something did flash in his eyes.

"Willing?" he asked slowly. Reaching behind him, he shut the door, ignoring that there was a crack in the wood where he'd—what, bashed it in?

"Yes," I swallowed. "Willing."

Liar.

"Bullshit," he said. "You didn't want him."

He stalked toward me, like a predator scenting its prey and playing with it.

"What do you mean?" I asked, raising my chin to hide how nervous—and excited—his pursuit was making me.

This time, a small, knowing smile played over Blake's face as he reached me and lifted a piece of my hair between his unbandaged fingers, stroking it. I couldn't even feel his touch, but the way my whole body quaked, I may as well have.

"You didn't want him," he repeated slowly. Confidently. "You just wanted to forget about how much you want me. Or you wanted my attention. Well, troublemaker. I'm here now, and you have it." The smile on his face disappeared. "Now, get on the goddamn bed."

"**W**hat?!" I gaped at him.

"One of these days, you're going to listen to me when I tell you to do something," he muttered. And then for the second time that day, I was being lifted into his arms and carried—this time face to face.

His expression was stern. More than stern. His bones were more prominent, his mouth drawn tight, like it was taking effort to remain stoic. But the forest of his green eyes were lit with fire.

"I never listen to what anyone tells me to do," I said automatically.

In response, he dropped me on the bed. I bounced.

"Blake, what are you—what is..." my heart was racing so fast, I was sure it would burst at any moment.

I pinched myself.

He was watching.

"You're not dreaming," he said. "This is real."

"Then you better tell me what the hell is happening," I said honestly. "Because I'm losing my mind here. This is like, a total 180 from every other interaction we've had..."

"No, it's not," he said. "Lucy..." he rubbed his face with his bandaged hand like he'd forgotten it was there. "You don't know what you do to me. Everything about you: your hair, your body, your face, your attitude...I've tried to resist your siren song for so long, but I can't anymore. The thought of you giving that untouched cunt to someone else..." he shook his head like a dog shaking off water and growled again, the sound making my thighs clench.

Oh god.

Oh god.

Oh—

"...I don't care if it makes me irresponsible, bad, is going to send me to hell. If you're so determined to get rid of your virginity, then I'll gladly take it from you."

"Oh," I gasped. He'd knocked the breath right out of me with that speech.

"Oh?"

He prowled toward the bed, kicking off his shoes and removing his jacket as he went. Part of me, most of me, couldn't believe it. It was everything I'd ever wanted.

But when he got on the bed and kneeled above me, beginning to unbutton the top of his black shirt, the gauze on his bandage beginning to come undone, another part of me woke up.

Yeah, he was all I'd ever wanted.

But that didn't mean he wasn't being a complete asshole and I wasn't *pissed*.

"You don't think this is presumptuous at all?" I said from the bed, looking up at him and trying to ignore the skin that was being revealed to me, skin I'd never seen before. "Maybe I wanted Sam. Maybe I don't want you. You don't get to follow me—how did you even find me?"

He didn't answer but kept watching me, stilling his hands.

"Whatever," I waved that away. "You don't get to follow me, ruin my plans, and force yourself into my life this way. You don't get to be a complete jackass and"—damn, I was about to be grossly vulnerable—"hurt my feelings and reject me and then sweep in like you belong here."

"You're right," he said simply. "I'm sorry. I was a jackass."

Yeah, he had been, but even though that simple apology deflated my sails a bit, it didn't diminish all my righteous fury.

"You were. Multiple times. You made me feel stupid and lonely and worthless, and I'm sick of it. And now you're cave-manning your way in here and claiming me—"

"You're right," he repeated, interrupting me, and then he was grabbing my hips, making my heart beat even faster, and lifting me up so I was also kneeling. "I am claiming you, and I am a jackass, and that doesn't matter, because you know what I realized tonight, Lucy?"

"What?" I hated how my voice trembled, but what was I supposed to do when his hands were stroking over the satin covering the dimples in my hips?

His eyes pierced me—through my body, my pussy, my heart. "That you're mine. You belong to me. And I clearly haven't been taking good care of what's mine, have I, troublemaker? Well, that stops *now*."

And then he released my hip with one big hand, gripped my hair, tugged my head back, and placed a kiss on my bare neck.

He'd avoided my lips, but his lips were doing some really talented work to my neck and my whole body went up in flames. I moaned, submitting, knowing better, knowing that if this didn't work out, if he changed his mind, it was going to hurt. And I didn't care.

I was Lucy Fucking Braverman.

I could handle anything.

And I was finally getting the thing I'd always dreamed about.

He released my neck, and I chased after his lips, but he turned his head away.

A splinter burrowed into my heart. Tiny, but painful all the same.

"You won't kiss me?" I asked, hating how small my voice sounded.

"Oh, I'll kiss you," he assured me. "But not there. I've got my control hanging by a thread and if I—I'll snap."

And then he was pushing me back down against the bed, and pulling up my dress, and I forgot all about him not kissing me on the lips.

Especially when he groaned like a lost, dying animal.

"Yeah, you're mine," he said, staring down at me. "And I'm about to show you—and this little pussy—how and why."

13

BLAKE

I couldn't kiss her. Not on her mouth.

I wanted to, oh god, I desperately wanted to. But I'd never kissed a woman on the mouth. When I was seven, my first foster father told me that kissing was only for people who deserved love.

I didn't deserve love. I knew nothing about it. Wasn't made for it. I was a poor foster kid from the wrong side of the tracks who'd lucked out with hockey. I didn't know *how*.

So I couldn't kiss Lucy, even if the temptation of her lips as they sought mine destroyed me. I'd fantasized about them for so long, they haunted my dreams. But if I let the little troublemaker kiss me, and she didn't mean it, there'd be no coming back from that. She was mine, but I also knew she was young and exploring, and as much as it killed me— and I'd almost killed that poor fucker over it—I may not be hers.

Call me a coward, call me a chump, but when this ended —and it would end—I needed to keep myself whole. So, no kissing on the lips.

But everywhere else?

Hell, I'd kiss her, bite her, mark her everywhere like the animal I apparently was.

Starting with the cunt that was calling to me and begging to be eaten.

Grabbing her dress by the waist, I pulled on the seams until it ripped open, revealing thick, round, curvy thighs and...

A bare, shaved cunt. No underwear, no nothing.

She hadn't had panty lines, but I hadn't considered she'd forgone underwear tonight.

And another man could've seen it.

"You bad girl," I told her as I unwrapped the bandage from around my hand. "You've been walking around like this all night? Nothing covering this sweet pussy?"

And before I could think better of it, remind myself that she was a virgin, I'd delivered a hard slap to her wet cunt, right over the clit that was already peeking out from underneath its hood, leaving blood behind. It wasn't quite the bloody handprint, but it would have to do.

Lucy *screamed.*

"That hurt?" I asked her in a low, thick voice that didn't sound like mine.

"Yes," she said on a moan. "It hurt so good."

"Good," I said. "Because you're never walking around like this again, where anyone can catch a glimpse of *my* pussy. You hear me, sweetheart? Or next time I *will* kill someone."

My pussy.

My everything.

Mine.

I delivered another slap for good measure, leaving another trail of blood. Her whole body rocked, wetness seeping out, sex and sunshine filling the air and making my cock so hard my slacks strangled it.

Lucy must have been watching it, because her eyes—those saucy, confident, take no prisoners eyes—grew round, dark, and hazy with desire.

"Yeah, he's hard for you, troublemaker." I murmured. "And I promise you're going to become intimately acquainted with him. But for now, daddy wants to eat."

I didn't know where the word came from, but when I'd heard her getting off and calling me that earlier, it stirred up something inside of me. It woke up something that had been sleeping for a long time, maybe forever. I wanted, no, *needed* to care for her, provide for her, and protect her in every way she needed, too.

"Daddy?" she whispered, and then shook her head like she was bringing reality back. Her voice flattened. "What, you think I have daddy issues or something?"

I snorted. "I *know* you have daddy issues. We both know I'm nothing like your father. Or any father. That's not what this is about. Right here, right now, I'm going to give you everything you want, even if you didn't know you wanted it. I'm going to take care of you, sweetheart, and yeah, that makes me your daddy in bed. And look," I swiped my thumb up the seam of her cunt, pleased with the wetness that covered it and the way she writhed underneath me from the touch. Not only pleased, completely unmoored by the soft silk of her skin. "Look," I repeated. "It's obvious you like it."

She blinked. She didn't need to know how I knew she had a daddy kink, she just needed to know we'd explore it together. Lifting my thumb to my lips, I sucked it into my mouth, tasting starlight, and the worst and best of sins.

And that thread, the very last thread holding my control together, snapped.

Wrenching her thighs apart, I lifted her up and wrapped her legs around my neck, dragging blood all over her skin and not giving a single fuck about it. No, not when angling her like this put me in the perfect position to get my mouth on her.

"Has anyone ever done this before?" I asked into her cunt, ready to go out and kill someone.

She shook her head. "No, no one's ever—"

Good enough.

I opened my mouth and licked her slit, tracing circles around but not on her clit, holding her tight while she squirmed.

"Still. Stay still," I reprimanded. "If you don't, I'll tie you up so you *can't* move."

"Oh fuck, Coach," she moaned.

I growled. "Not Coach. Not here. What do you call me when I'm licking your pussy?"

I waited, breathing on her and watching her try to twist away from the air from my lungs blowing over her clit.

"Daddy..."

"Yes, that's it. That's right. Good girl," I praised and continued to lick her.

She liked that. Wetness poured out of her.

"What are you doing, you can't..." she moaned again.

"Shhh, sweetheart," I murmured. "Don't tell me I can't. Don't tell me anything right now. Daddy's eating, and he doesn't want any interruptions."

I bent my head back down, sucking on one lip of her pussy, then the other, biting gently for now, before making my way back up to her mound. I pressed kisses and bites and sucked on the soft, vulnerable skin, distantly aware I was going to leave marks and bruises but not caring. Distantly aware that this wasn't how you treated a virgin. But based on the moans and whimpers coming out of that succulent mouth I wanted but couldn't have, the little troublemaker didn't care, either.

I'd eaten a lot of pussy in my life. Men who avoided it weren't men, but fucking idiots. Sometimes it tasted good, sometimes not so good. But this? Lucy's cunt was more delicious than the juiciest of steaks, sweeter than the flourless chocolate cake I loved, richer than the reddest of wines. I could eat her and lick her forever, and never, ever need anything else. Especially as her swollen clit prodded my lower lip.

She was ready for me.

Moving my mouth a little lower, I stroked my tongue—gently at first—over it, delighted as it pulsed against my tongue. I was ecstatic as a high, feral groan sounded above me, making me look up from what I was doing.

"Feels good, sweetheart?"

"I thought I wasn't—supposed to—talk," she sassed on short, gasping breaths.

Oh, this troublemaker. I grinned against her.

"You can answer me when I ask you questions. But the sassing—well, troublemakers who sass get punished for it."

Capturing her clit between my lips, I bit down, firm but not hard, rewarded by how her whole body froze, then shook. Her release filled my mouth, so sweet and succulent and rich, drenching me. I continued to work her clit between my teeth and tongue, holding her hips tight, listening as she cried out:

"Daddy, daddy, oh god, daddy," as she came.

The sounds of her cries were even sweeter than she tasted.

"That's right," I murmured, pressing a small kiss to her trembling clit, wishing it was her lips, and watching the glazed daze in her eyes as she continued to come. "Daddy... god...either works. Do you know how hard you've made me, tasting you this way? I'm gonna fuck this pussy so hard."

"Please, please, please," she begged.

"Not yet," I said, in that same unfamiliar voice. But then nothing about myself was familiar at this point. I didn't know who I'd become, but with the taste and smell of Lucy all over my lips and face, I didn't give a shit. Later, there'd be regret and recriminations, and maybe that extended visit to the police precinct. For now, there was only Lucy: blood-stained thighs trapped in my hands, lying underneath me, pupils blown with desire and need. Desperate for me. Only for me, because she was mine.

For now, she was mine.

The knowledge that she might not be forever made me grip her thighs tighter, likely leaving bruises. "You can give daddy a few more, can't you?" I asked, not waiting for an answer when I dove back in, this time pointing my tongue and aiming it between her pussy lips so I could taste even more of her from the inside. And oh, fuck. Oh fuck, but she was so goddamn tight, her walls clenching around my tongue as I thrust it inside, sweeping it around, licking up everything I could find, playing with her. If she gripped my tongue that tight, what would she do to my cock?

My cock pulsed, balls hard and heavy like boulders, complaining because they wanted in on the action.

Lucy was crying, whimpering, screaming above me, staring at me with begging and unbelieving eyes as I stabbed and poked at the inside of her. Her clit was fat, red, swollen now, begging for more. Because my tongue couldn't be in two places at once, I released one of her thighs.

"Do not move," I ordered, and used my free hand to push a finger into her cunt, returning my tongue to her desperate, needy, hard little clit.

Fuck, so tight. So perfect.

For me.

And only for me.

I didn't realize I'd spoken out loud until I heard her repeating, "only for you,"—the three most satisfying words I'd ever heard in the English language.

I replaced one finger with two, turning and curving them so I could reach her g-spot and rub while I licked her clit in relentless circles, triumphant when her cunt started spasming around those two fingers, watching as desperate pleasure made its way across Lucy's face.

"Too much," she whimpered.

"Then it's perfect," I corrected, not easing up, not giving her a break, as I continued to stroke her from the inside with my finger and the outside with my tongue, watching and listening as she fell over the cliff into her third, fourth, and fifth orgasms.

By the sixth, she'd fully submitted, lax against me, a ragdoll on the bed as she begged and warbled and whimpered nonsense. Begging me to stop, begging for more, begging for less.

She'd also loosened up quite a bit. Enough that my cock, ready to throw a mutiny, could finally get its turn.

Releasing her legs, I leaned down, capturing her trembling chin between my thumb and forefinger and lifting it so I could stare into her eyes.

Tears poured out, concerning me for a moment.

"Sweetheart, I didn't hurt you, did I?"

"You did," she whimpered, before begging, "Do it again."

Triumphant, I gripped her chin harder. "Say please."

"Please."

"Please, who?"

She stared up at me, submissive and compliant for maybe the first time in her life.

"Do it again. Please, daddy," she said. "I dare you."

A brutal grin split my face. "Do you, troublemaker? Can you come again?"

I didn't let her answer that as I undid my belt, unbuttoned my slacks, and pushed them down my legs, not even bothering to remove them the whole way. My cock had already forced its way over the top of my boxer briefs, and I pushed those down, too, letting it free, where it bobbed against my stomach.

"Oh, shit," Lucy had recovered enough to stare. "There's no way in hell you're going to fit."

"Oh, I'll fit," I told her. "Daddy's fat cock will fit *just* fine. You know how I know?"

She shook her head.

"I know, because this greedy little cunt is begging for it."

"This greedy little cunt is tired," she sassed.

"Is that so? Then there are other holes I can use."

She licked her lips, and god, it was tempting to use that mouth a different way if I wasn't going to kiss it. But I had a purpose, and that siren of a cunt was calling to me, tired or not.

I lifted one of her legs, throwing it over my arm to open her up to me, pulling her down the bed, and grabbed my cock with my other hand. I was soaked in precum, and it would take everything in me not to blow the second I got inside her. But I was going to enjoy this for as long as possible.

In case it never happens again, because it can't, that dick of an inner voice pointed out. I banished it to the depths of hell that were waiting for me.

But first, heaven.

I contented myself by teasing her at first, slapping her cunt with the head of my cock, then using it to draw circles over her clit. Lucy's eyes were transfixed, especially when I aimed lower and pushed—just an inch, just the tip—inside.

And groaned. Because I'd been right—heaven.

Intent on not hurting her, I stayed where I was, obsessed with the way the wet heat of her kissed the skin of my cock, like it was inviting me into the best home in existence. A home I'd never expected.

I'd never had a home. Not really.

But there was no time for morose bullshit, not when I'd found the most perfect home in the world.

I began to push in a little deeper, until I hit resistance.

Oh, fuck.

Most women didn't have a hymen, especially not one as physically active as Lucy. But here it was, evidence that she really was only mine.

"Oh sweetheart, this might hurt," I warned. "But then it's going to feel so good."

Playing with her hard little clit, I pulled back slowly—

And then thrust inside, breaking past that last bit of resistance, and straight into nirvana. I pushed deeper, and deeper still, gripped on all sides by her little cunt, obsessed with the way it both fought me and tried to swallow me at the same time. Each centimeter was a revelation, her walls tight around the ridges of my cock.

Yes, this was my new home.

And I was never, ever fucking leaving.

14

LUCY

Oh god.

Was pain supposed to feel this good?

Blake rested his arm on one side of me, the other still holding my left leg open. He was deep inside me, so deep I could feel him everywhere, practically splitting me open with how big his cock was. And he was still rubbing circles on my clit, sending sparks of pleasure—incomparable, impossible pleasure—inside me.

I felt so full. Surrounded. My eyes drifted shut from the feeling, needing to imprint it on my brain, how good it felt. I mean, I knew it would feel good to get what I always wanted, but I hadn't imagined *this*.

"No, you look at me, little troublemaker," Blake said, his low voice rumbling through me. "You watch me while I fuck you."

My eyes shot open. His were...oh, I didn't know how to describe them. Usually, he seemed so closed off from me, from everyone, but they were wide and expressive, with exultant ownership in them.

"Blake," I whined. "I need—"

"I know what you need," he murmured, leaning down to drop a kiss on my hair, surprisingly gentle for how huge he was inside me. "I think I've always known what you needed."

As my heart tripped over his words, he lifted his hips, pulling his cock out as my own tried to chase his and keep him inside me.

He chuckled. "Oh, sweetheart, you think we're done?"

And then he thrust back inside me, *hard*.

Little explosions went off in my brain.

"Not quite," he murmured, changing his angle before pulling back out and thrusting back in.

That time, he hit something inside me that turned the little explosions into detonations.

"That's it," he said, grinning, and then he was stroking in and out, hard and fast and strong. The feeling was a revelation, a million, trillion times better than any fantasy I'd ever had of him. He stared down at me, his hard face spread in near ecstasy as he worked me over and over and over, urging me to—

"Come again, sweetheart. Go tight and come all over my cock like you came all over my tongue and fingers earlier. Squeeze my cock tight and drench it, I know you can do it. I know you want to. Show daddy who owns you."

"Oh god, I can't," I moaned. The precipice was approaching, but the abyss below it scared me. So far, each time I'd come, I'd become more and more vulnerable, showing Blake parts of my soul I'd sworn to keep to myself. What would happen if I came again? Would I shatter into pieces only to never be put back together?

He shook his head. "You're Lucy Braverman. You can do anything you want to. And right now, you want to come, don't you, sweetheart? Won't it feel good, letting go with my thick, fat cock inside you? Won't it feel good, squeezing it so tight I have no choice but to come in you?"

Oh, shit. Condom.

"Blake," I started.

He must have caught where I was going, because he shook his head. "I know you have an IUD, Lucy. And you don't have to worry about me."

How did he know?

"Wha—"

"Haven't fucked anyone in a long ass time," he said. "Hadn't wanted to."

Hope, insidious and foolish, flared.

"Why?"

He thrust again.

"Because," he said, the words wrenched out of him like he had no interest in confessing. "None of them were you. Now, *come.*"

I did, his words tripping me as I fell into the precipice, his cock so hard and thick inside me, his thumb still working my clit, playing me like a harp as my whole body tensed and released and all I could see was Blake's eyes. An unholy cry came out of me, the orgasm stretching out as Blake thrust hard and fast, rhythm uncontrolled as he threw his head back, shouting my name as he came, wet heat filling me up and up and up, sending me over the edge one last time.

I'd been right.

With one last groan, Blake pulled out of me, watching as his come and mine spilled out onto the bed. I looked down at the smear of blood across my pussy from his cut hand. *He* looked down at his cock, only starting to soften, and the blood ringing it.

And then he shocked me when he swiped a finger over it.

"Open," he said.

I did, and he pushed his finger into my mouth, making me taste copper and cum, him and me.

And then he was removing his finger, swiping it over his cock again, and licking it up himself.

Shutting his eyes, he groaned. "Fuck, I thought nothing would taste better than your cunt, but nothing beats the taste of knowing you're mine."

He leaned over, like he was about to kiss me, making my heart flutter, but at the last minute, he moved his mouth, kissing my ear.

"Thank you, sweetheart," he said. "I'm a bad man, and you let me be that man."

And with that, he lifted me into his arms, carrying me toward the bathroom where I could only lie there, limply, smelling us together, elated and broken.

I'd been right.

I was shattered into pieces, and I'd never be the same.

Especially because he still hadn't kissed me.

15

BLAKE

What the fuck had I done?

As I sat in the hot bath with Lucy in my arms, slowly washing her body as she rested half asleep against me, the regret and recriminations spilled out.

I'd just fucked my ward.

Taken her virginity.

Made her eighteen-year-old pussy come all over me. Just thinking about that made me harden all over again, because I'd clearly turned into a teenager, both with the can-always-go dick, and the apparently undeveloped prefrontal cortex. What else could explain my decisions tonight?

It was my job to care for her. It had always been my job to care for her, and I'd shirked my duties. And now here we were, me having done the worst possible thing I could think of. Lucy's makeup had run down her face, and even though she was tall for a woman, she was so small in my arms. So delicate. I could hurt her so easily. I'd done a terrible thing, and I didn't know how to come back from it.

And I didn't think I wanted to.

My cock thought she was ours. That we'd done the right thing, claiming her this way. But I'd seen the pain in her eyes when I hadn't kissed her, and I still couldn't bring myself to. It was like by protecting myself from that one intimacy, I could pretend I hadn't done something horrible. It was bullshit, I knew, probably even worse, but here we were.

I murmured to her, humming, as I brushed a soapy washcloth over her chest, her arms, her tits, her stomach. When I worked it down toward her pussy, she shifted in my arms.

"Too sensitive," she complained.

"Too bad," I responded, gently cleaning her off, as much as I wanted to let my claim—both blood and cum—dry all over her. When we'd talked about the IUD, a small, fucked-up part of me regretted it, wanting to claim her even more fully. But I knew better. I'd already done enough to hurt her, getting her pregnant would actually destroy her life in ways I was unwilling to do. And I was grateful, because the IUD meant we hadn't needed a condom to separate us.

She shivered in my arms, the water turning cool. Lifting her out of the tub, I carried her back onto the tile, grabbing a fluffy towel and drying her off, gentle and slow, admiring every naked curve I'd never seen before. I'd been so desperate to get my mouth on her and then get inside her, I hadn't bothered to get her naked. Seeing her bare tits, the swell to her stomach, her pale, perfect skin—well, she was a goddamn miracle. No woman, living or dead, could compare.

"Do you regret it?" she murmured.

She could read me too well.

I kissed her forehead.

"No," I said, because I didn't regret it. Regretting it would mean regretting *her*. I regretted myself and my actions, period.

She gifted me with a smile as bright as the sun, before yawning.

"Alright, troublemaker. Time for bed." I dried off too, rewrapping the bandage around my hand, and then lifted her again, carrying her back into the bedroom and placing her gently on the bed, staring down at her.

"Don't leave me," she pleaded.

"Like I could," I said gruffly, sliding under the covers and pulling her into my arms, trying to ignore my horny cock getting the wrong message.

"No more," she said, also feeling it.

I kissed her hair, breathing her sunshine-and-sex scent into my lungs. Memorizing it, so I could recall it whenever I needed to. I had a feeling I would need to often.

"No more," I promised. "For now."

As she drifted to sleep, and I held her perfect, vulnerable yet strong body in my imperfect, asshole arms, the truth echoed in my head.

Because it shouldn't have been "no more for now."

It should've been no more—forever.

16

LUCY

I woke up thinking about wedding colors.

My wedding colors, to be specific.

Barbie Pink—my signature color—was probably a little too on the nose and didn't really go well with anything other than gold or white, which might be a little gaudy, even for me. Nor did I think I could get Blake into a Barbie Pink tuxedo, as hot as that would be—and damn, it would be hot.

I sighed, eyes closed, warm in the hotel sheets and under the duvet, relaxed and happy and...for the first time since I was a little girl and maybe since forever...feeling like I finally *belonged.*

Mine, he'd said.

And yes, I was his.

Even if he hadn't kissed me.

At that, my eyes shot open. We were going to change that right now.

I shifted over, turning to look at him, ready to plant a kiss on his lips, morning breath and all...

Except no one was there.

There was no one in the bed beside me.

The sheets were a little rumpled and the pillow was slightly indented. I was in the hotel room, he had been here with me, I hadn't imagined it—I had the sore, raw pussy to prove it.

So where was he?

Dread wanted to set up camp in my stomach, but I wouldn't let the squatter in. Blake had to be here somewhere. He wouldn't leave, would he? Wouldn't abandon the girl whose virginity he'd taken the night before...

Rolling out of bed and trying to ignore the way my inner thighs ached, I wandered over to the bathroom, throwing open the door.

No one was there.

I stepped out, circling the room, inanely going to the closet door and opening that, too, in case he was—what, Lucy, hiding in there?

I was being an idiot.

A foolish, *foolish*, hopeful little girl.

Because the writing was clear as day.

Even clearer when I spotted the pad of paper on the desk next to the closet.

Shutting my eyes, I bargained with myself, with the universe, with whatever was out there—maybe it would say *ran out for black coffee for me and one of those disgusting skinny mocha lattes for you—do you know how much sugar is in one of those? Back in a few.*

But I knew better. Lifting the pad of paper with a shaking hand, I glanced at the writing—big, bold, block letters, solid and confident, even when they said things like:

I'M SORRY, LUCY. YOU DESERVE BETTER THAN THIS.

COACH SAMSON

That was it.

That was all it said.

He'd even signed it formally, like we'd never been intimate.

I sank to the floor, my ass thudding on the carpet, wrapping my legs in my arms and burying my head in my knees. Which was worse, the hurt, or knowing I'd set myself up for it?

I never should've let him fuck me.

I never should've fucked him.

I should've kicked him out, chased down Sam, made sure he was alright. Should've realized how wrong things were when Blake refused to kiss me. Should've known that I, Lucy Braverman, wasn't meant for a happily ever after.

No wedding colors for me.

I never cried, but tears welled up in my eyes and I let them loose, wetting my bare, naked knees. I shivered in my own arms as I let out all the pain—not just from this morning, but from the last six years. I'd been alone for so long, and part of me—the part of me I didn't even share with therapists, because I knew they'd blame "abandonment issues" —believed I didn't deserve anything better.

At that thought, my tears paused.

Because yes, I might feel that way.

But I knew it wasn't true.

Mine, Blake's voice echoed in my head.

Okay, so he was technically a grown ass man. But he was also a coward. And I could let him be a coward. I could nurse my wounds and then go out in the world, minus one hymen (who knew I even still had one?) and with a little more knowledge, and find other men to fuck or maybe even to love me. But that wasn't what I wanted, and I, Lucy Braverman, never hid from what I wanted. No, if I wanted to jump fifty feet into cold water late at night, I did it. If I wanted to wear a tiny skirt to a hockey game knowing I'd get shit for it, I did it.

And if I wanted a man? Well, I was going to make him mine.

I needed to be clever, creative, stubborn, and determined —all things I already was.

Ideas bubbled up in my brain, and for the first time since I'd discovered Blake had left, I smiled, wiping away my tears.

"This is gonna be fun," I murmured to myself.

I was going to bring that man to his knees. And then he was going to crawl to me and beg for forgiveness on those same knees.

And who knew? Maybe after he'd groveled enough, I'd forgive him.

Maybe.

17

BLAKE

"What the fuck has gotten into you? And what the hell did you do to your hand?"

Trey stood in front of me, hands on his hips, glaring.

On the ice, our team was in the middle of a bag skate. More than one player had paused to puke.

It was only 7:00 a.m., and I'd called for an emergency practice at 5:00, citing disappointment in their performance. It was complete bullshit. I was angry—mostly at myself—and decided to take it out on the team. It was a dick move, but it was a day of dick moves for me.

If I shut my eyes, even for one moment, I could picture Lucy asleep in bed, her head nuzzling the pillow I'd been using, dreaming peacefully—probably expecting I'd be there in the morning when she woke. I could just as easily picture her yawning, stretching, reaching for me—only to realize I wasn't there.

I was an asshole. But staying would've been worse. I'd been so caught up in the smell of her, the taste of her, and seeing another man with his hands on her, that I'd temporarily lost my mind, lost all control, and behaved heinously.

What the hell was I doing, fucking someone half my age, taking a young woman's virginity, *hurting* her with my demanding body and cock, making her bleed and bruise, covering her with my own blood, and taking advantage of the one person I was supposed to protect?

Shouldn't I be protecting her from disgusting men like me?

"Are you going to answer me?"

Trey watched my face, shaking his head. He wasn't backing off.

I shrugged.

"It's good for the team. And don't worry about my hand." I'd cleaned it again and re-bandaged it. It stung a little, a reminder of how unhinged I'd gotten the night before.

"Is it good for the team?" he rolled his eyes. "Or do you have demons you can't exorcise so you're trying to take them out on these kids? Because they've been running drills for two hours and today is supposed to be a day off for them."

"There aren't days off when we need to win," I pointed out, even though his words hit their target.

I *was* taking my demons out on these kids. I was frustrated, I wanted to be back in bed with Lucy, I wanted to be the kind of man who didn't care about the consequences of my actions. But I did, and I wasn't, and so here we were.

Trey shook his head, opening his mouth to retort, when we heard whistling.

I turned my head toward the noise and froze.

Because there she was.

Whatever a walk of shame was, this was the opposite. It was like everything had stopped in time, and there was only her. I started from her feet and scanned up, partially to reassure myself she was okay, but mostly because I wasn't ready to look her in the eye and see how much I'd hurt her.

Her toes peeked out of those flip flops I hated—a dare, a fuck you. Her legs were bare, shapely, solid, and as my eyes traveled up and up, I saw one hip jutted out, covered—just barely—by a short pink, orange, and white plaid skirt which barely hid her pussy from me. From everyone. I caught the growl in my throat. Her stomach was a bare, pale gold, and even though I'd seen her in crop tops so many times, seeing naked skin reminded me of last night in the bath, her skin wet and shining, when she'd been wrapped in my arms in the tub. Skin I'd pressed kisses all over. A little crop top—of course—covered her tits, but she wasn't wearing a bra, and I could see her areolas through it. Rose-colored. I knew now.

And if I could see them, so could every other goddamn person on the rink.

This time, I couldn't contain the growl.

Trey's head whipped toward me. Hell, everyone's did—the growl echoed so loudly through the arena, the only sound that had been made since trouble came walking back in.

I continued my perusal, up past her breasts—breasts I hadn't paid enough attention to the night before, and damn, did I want to rectify that now—to her neck.

My eyes lit on something, and breath whooshed out of me.

A hickey.

I'd given her a fucking hickey.

And she wasn't even hiding it. I'd claimed her there, and all I wanted was to bite all the way around her neck until she wore a collar of bruises from my teeth, a signal to every other man in the universe to stay away.

The hickey was a proclamation. Not that she belonged

to me, no. That she wasn't ashamed of what had happened the night before. But when did Lucy ever feel shame? She was the opposite of me in that way, and I'd always admired her for it, even if it made me want to rip my hair out at the roots.

It was the look on her face that did me in. Her lips, succulent and sweet and begging for my cock between them, begging me to *kiss* them, were quirked in a small smile, like she knew something I didn't.

Like that something she knew was *me*.

And her eyes, oh her eyes. They swallowed me up and spat me right back out. I was lacking, a coward, and didn't even deserve retribution and rage. No, I was too below her for that.

I see you, they said. *And I think you're full of shit.*

And she, the goddess, was right. No one that young should be that wise, but Lucy had always seen through people's bullshit, and today the bullshit was mine.

She looked like a naughty student seducing her professor. She looked like any man's wet dream. She looked like jailbait.

Trey whistled, and my hand fisted at my side. It was the only way I could keep myself from punching my assistant coach in the fucking throat. I'd kicked enough men's asses as it was.

Control, Blake. Control. Your middle fucking name, and don't you forget it.

Flanking Lucy was her entourage: Leslie, my center's fiancée, with her dark hair and bemused eyes, stood to one side. Tovah and Aviva, two troublemakers-in-waiting at our rival school, Reina University, stood on her other, arms crossed and grinning. Tovah whispered something in Aviva's ear, and shit, these girls knew. As much as that could fuck with my entire career, I was glad that Lucy had friends to confide in. That she wasn't alone.

Alone like you left her early this morning, my brain supplied.

Finally, Lucy opened that delectable trouble of a mouth.

"Hi boys," she called. "What did I miss?"

There were catcalls in response.

"Coach is trying to kill us," Emory said.

"Did you ever find that panty stealer?" another one of my players called.

I tried not to fist my hand in my pocket. I'd been carrying her panties around for days—like they were my good luck charm.

"No," she said, laughing. "But I appreciate the concern." To me, she pursed her lips. "Don't you think you're being a little...hard on them?"

Her "hard" sang in the air, and even though no one else picked up the implication, I did.

"It must be...frustrating," she added. "And a little bit cruel."

She shrugged her shoulders and tossed that long, blonde hair. Hair that had been spread out on a pillow beneath me as she'd whimpered, moaned, and cried out my name last night.

Hair that I suddenly wanted to cover up so no one else could see the gorgeous golds and yellows. Once again, I fantasized about convincing her to wear a wig so no one could see her hair but me.

"It's okay, boys," she said. "I believe in you. You're all tough and brave men, and you can handle this. In fact," her eyes turned wicked, and she winked—at me. "I'm happy to give a massage to whoever stays standing the longest. No puking."

There was a chorus of "yes ma'am" and whistles, and then my team started skating harder, longer, faster, wanting to impress the blonde vixen in front of them who was trying to kill me with her disdain and disinterest.

"No massages," I barked. "No fraternizing, you all know the rules." *Or I'll kick you off the team or kick your asses.*

"Oh, but Coach," she said sweetly, her eyes promising pure hell. "Rules are made to be broken."

She blew a kiss at the team. With my eagle eye vision, I spotted it, a tell: One nail—just one—looked bitten to the quick, the only sign that she'd been upset. Lucy had bitten her nails as a kid, and I'd thought she'd broken the habit, but she wasn't as unaffected as she seemed.

I had hurt her. I'd abandoned her this morning and no matter how brave and strong she was being right now, the truth of what I'd done to her was a hard pill to swallow.

"Bye, boys. Have a good practice, and I promise I'll see you later," she said, unaware that I'd spotted it.

With that, she pivoted and walked out, skirt molded to her ass, hips swaying, her friends trailing after her.

It took every ounce of restraint to not move toward her, throw her over my shoulder in a fireman's carry, take her to my office, and swat that ass bright red until she begged for mercy and promised to never get near my players ever again. Then I imagined tying her down and eating her pussy again...

I stopped my daydream just in time. Before I destroyed her reputation, and mine.

"Oh, that's what's going on," Trey observed. "Fuck."

I didn't answer him.

Even though "fuck" was right.

18

LUCY

"**F**uck, that felt good," I sighed once we reached the outside of the athletic center.

Tovah, Aviva, and Leslie surrounded me.

"Are you going to tell us what's going on?" Leslie asked.

"Only if you swear that this stays here," I told her.

As angry as I was, I didn't want this to get out. It could destroy my reputation—and Coach's career. He'd get fired for sleeping with a student, and no one would want anything to do with either of us. It was too taboo.

And then there was Professor Putrovski to consider. Would she still write me a recommendation letter if she knew I'd slept with the man she wanted?

Fuck.

"Of course it stays here," Leslie said.

Aviva rolled her eyes. "You know we're good at keeping secrets."

"Maybe too good," Tovah added, elbowing her.

"Like you can talk," Aviva retorted.

Leslie raised her hand. "I can guess." She turned to me. "You fucked him, didn't you?"

Immediately, memories from the night before replayed in my mind. The feeling of him in between my legs, his eyes watching me, his cock making me so full, the *mine*, the way he held me...

I raised my chin. "Well, I'm not a virgin anymore, I'll say that much."

Leslie grinned. "I told you so. I knew you weren't over him." But when she saw my face, her own fell.

"Oh, no. That whole production was because he was an asshole, wasn't he?"

I wasn't going to lie about it. "The biggest asshole ever. Abandoned me in the middle of the night with some bull-shit note," I said, rifling through my purse and handing it over to her because I'd already memorized it.

Tovah shook her head. "I'll kill him for you," she offered. "I know someone who can help us hide the body. I mean, I'm engaged to someone who can help us hide the body..."

I shook my head, knowing she was telling the truth. "We can't kill him. We're only a few games away from making the playoffs. The team would never forgive me if he died, and I don't think Trey is a good enough coach to get them where they need to be."

Tovah and Aviva glanced at each other. "Okay, well then..."

I interrupted. "I don't want to kill him. I want to make him regret walking out on me. Every single nanosecond of every single day, until he comes crawling back on his knees and begging, maybe then I'll forgive him and let him fuck me again."

"I love you," Leslie said, admiration in her voice.

"So what's the plan?"

"Does Jack still have access to Vice and Vixen?" I asked Aviva, referencing her own fiancé.

Vice and Vixen were two black market sex aphrodisiacs that were dealt around Tabb and Reina. Well, Vice was sort of like Viagra—on steroids. Vixen was more like a roofie and really fucked with people with XX chromosomes. It used to run rampant around both campuses until recently.

Aviva shook her head. "The team got out of that game after shit went so haywire. They still know who's dealing, but I don't think they have easy access. It's not on campus anymore."

Tovah cleared her throat. "I can get it. You want Vice, right?"

"What haven't you told me?" Aviva accused.

"You can get it?" I asked.

Tovah nodded. "I know where to source it. I need to warn you though—even for a man as big as Coach Samson, that shit is potent. And it'll turn him feral. Like, completely out of control. Make sure you're ready for the responsibility of that—and the consequences."

Feral, out of control, that was exactly what I wanted. The only time he was honest was when he snapped. I didn't just need his body, I wanted all of him on board, and even though it was bad, even though I knew it was wrong...well, a girl had to do what a girl had to do.

"I want it," I said.

"Oh, shit," Leslie muttered.

I grinned.

It felt good to be bad.

♥.♥

A WEEK LATER, I WALKED INTO THE ATHLETIC ADMINISTRATION building, heading up the stairs toward Blake's office. In my purse was a little vial of Vice. I had a mission, and no one and nothing would deter me from it.

Fortunately, Trey wasn't around, and Blake never locked his office door. He really needed to start doing that. And not leave his water bottle sitting out. He was just...

Just asking for it, Lucy?

Oh, shit.

I froze where I stood, in front of his desk, about to uncork the small vial of Vice Tovah had gotten for me and pour it in his water.

I sank into his chair, placing the vial gently on his desk and burying my head in my hands for the second time that day.

This was bad.

Like, there was bad, and there was *give the man you were obsessed with Viagra without him knowing* bad. Sure, Mason might have done it to Leslie, and from what I'd guessed, Jack had done something similar to Aviva, but I couldn't be that person. I couldn't take his choice away from him. I was so desperate for his affection, that I was willing to—what?— take away his choice? Fuck him without his real consent? Turn him into an animal and steal the one thing he absolutely needed: his control?

Rising out of the chair, I wiped away another tear—the second time that week I'd cried.

"I'm sorry," I whispered to the empty room. I was sorry for having even thought of it.

I went to open the door, and slammed right into a big, warm wall.

Craning my neck, I stared back at a pissed off Coach.

"Lucy, what the hell are you doing in my office?" he barked.

I shook my head. "I—"

I was never at a loss for words, but what was I supposed to tell him?

The truth, my conscience offered.

He stepped in the office, pushing me further inside, and locked the door behind him.

"Sit down and answer me," he ordered.

I hovered, hesitant for the first time in my life.

"Lucy, I swear to god, if you don't tell me what is going on...are you okay? Did someone do something to you? Why do you look so upset?"

Oh, that was *bullshit.*

"What do you think happened to me, asshole? *You* happened. You didn't have to come to the hotel that night." I swallowed. "You didn't have to interrupt me with that guy from the bar. You didn't have to fuck me, or call me yours, or—"

He raised a hand. "You're right. You're completely right. I'm sorry. I don't know what else to do, but if I could go back, if I could erase the whole night..."

I jerked like he'd shot me. Oh god, that hurt. It took everything in me not to let my chin tremble from his words. He regretted me that much?

He saw my reaction, because he reached for me. I stepped out of his way, refusing to let him touch me.

"Fuck, Lucy." He shook his head. "No, you misunderstand me. If I could go back, if I could erase the whole night, I'd do it the same way all over again." His lip quirked, although he looked better. "It makes me the worst kind of man, but I don't regret a second of it. All I regret is hurting you—and staying away from you for so long."

"Oh."

The wind went out of my sails. I wasn't angry, I wasn't...

anything. Other than guilty, because I'd almost done something I couldn't go back on.

Thank god I'd changed my mind.

"Is that why you came to my office, Lucy?" he said. "Because even though I don't regret it, I refuse to hurt you again..." he trailed off. "What's that in your hand?"

Oh, shit.

I tried to hide the vial, but he was too fast, crossing the room and bending down to swoop it out from between my fingers.

I stood up to grab it but he lifted it above my head, and when I stood on my tip toes, desperate, and reached, he grabbed one wrist, then the other, and forced them behind my back.

A whimper released from my throat. Him gripping me this way, keeping me still, the force behind it...god, I'd always wanted a man to use force on me like this. *This* man.

What was ironic was I'd basically tried to do the same thing to him.

He swirled the vial around, then popped the small cork and sniffed. Then threw back his head and laughed, shocking me.

"You were going to drug me with Vice? That was your big plan? Throw how little you cared in my face last week and then sneak it into a beverage so I was none the wiser? So you'd make me hard and horny for you, unable to keep my hands off you? My cock out of your holes? Make me lose my mind? Let me tell you something, troublemaker."

As he spoke, he was walking me backward, until my back hit the wall next to his bookcase, my arms trapped behind me. He loomed over me, swirling the Vice around.

"Vixen and Vice work differently. Vixen is like a roofie

on speed—it makes women lose time and place and forget everything, including their own names, completely mastered by their own libidos. But that's not how Vice works. If a man takes it…it makes him hyper conscious of every moment. Removes control, so he's mastered by who and what he wants, so goddamn hard and obsessed all rational thought flies out the window. But here's the thing—you don't need Vice for me, sweetheart. I'm already hard for you—" he pushed his hips against my stomach, so I could feel just how hard, and another whimper escaped my mouth.

"Already horny, already obsessed, barely able to keep my hands off you. I've been a bad, bad man, because all I've been able to think about for days is what it'll be like to shove my cock in all your holes. That tight pussy *I* broke in." His eyes went dark at that. "Between those lips that were meant to wrap around my cock, and give that sassy mouth something else to do. Work my way into that tight, virgin ass, and own you every single fucking way. Make you scream for me, and plant myself inside you so deep you couldn't get rid of me if you tried. Fuck, Lucy. You really think that Vice will make a difference?"

I could barely breathe from the images he was presenting to me. I wanted that, wanted all of that, but mostly—

"And why should I let you?" I said.

He raised an eyebrow. "Isn't that why you're here? Not to let me, but to *make* me?"

"I mean, yeah," I said. "But I *shouldn't.*"

"No, you shouldn't," he agreed. "You should get the hell out of here, fight me off, and run far, far away. Go report me to the dean, to the police, for being the worst thing that ever happened to you. Because I promise you, Lucy, I *am* the worst thing to ever happen to you—even if you're the best thing that's ever happened to me."

"What?" my voice was barely a whisper.

"Oh, yeah. You've ruined me by merely existing. But you made my boring life worth living again when you walked back into it. I've tried to stay away, tried to be a better man, but you don't want a better man, do you? No, you don't want the man—you want the out-of-control animal ravaging you. Well, sweetheart, you're about to get your wish."

He released my wrists.

"Lift your skirt," he ordered.

"Wha—"

"Lucy, if you're in my office, if you want this, we're doing things *my* way. I may lose control with you, but I'm in charge. I'm going to push you in ways you aren't ready for, and if you aren't okay with that, leave now and find a little boy to play with—if I don't kill him first. I'm giving you five seconds."

He began to count down. I planted my feet. Yeah, he was scaring me a bit, but I was excited. I wasn't going anywhere.

I lifted my skirt before he reached three.

"At least you're wearing panties this time," he muttered. Then: "Take them off."

Lifting one leg and then the other, I wriggled them down.

"Hand them over."

I placed them in his hand.

He lifted them to his nose and smelled, making my eyes narrow.

"Did you just—"

But he popped open the vial and, placing the gusset of my panties over his mouth, he opened it and poured the

Vice into it, sucking it out of my panties, not taking his eyes off me.

"What the fuck are you doing?"

"If I already feel this out of control when I see your naked cunt," he said when he was done, "Let's find out if you can handle me when I've forgotten how to spell the word."

Throwing my wet—no, wetter—panties on his desk, he checked his watch.

"It takes about half an hour to an hour to kick in," he said. "I'm already hard, but I think we're going to pass the time with you learning how to suck my cock the way I like it while you play with your pussy." He narrowed his eyes at me. "But, Lucy? No coming, or there will be consequences."

Shit, this wasn't what I'd said I wanted—I wanted him on his knees, crawling, begging for forgiveness. Not me on mine...but it turned me on too much to say no.

Still.

"And if I say no?"

He chuckled. "You can have a safeword. Use it if you need it, and then everything stops."

He stared me in the eyes. "Your safeword is guardian. Now, get on those cute little knees and open your mouth for daddy."

I looked him in the eyes. "Coach me, daddy."

"Ah, fuck," he groaned. "You're perfect, you know that, right? Dangerously so."

Perfect. I'd been many things in my life, but perfect had never been one of them.

Glowing from his praise, I kneeled down, my pussy bare to the air in his office, eyes trapped by his. He dropped the vial on the ground, kicking it under his desk. Coach was meticulously organized to the point of being fussy, and to see him so casual...well, it did more to me than I expected.

Maybe I was making him lose control. It made me feel powerful in ways I had never felt powerful before. Having the ability to make this man forget himself made me feel like a sex goddess, even if he hadn't called me one.

A submissive goddess, because he pointed to his pants and said, "Unzip me."

I reached out a hand, but he shook his head.

"Hands behind your back. Do it with your teeth."

Shit.

Pursing my lips, I searched for the zipper pull, and then, gently, I took it between my teeth and lowered my head and chin until it unzipped.

"Take me out," he said.

"Um."

His smile was almost gentle. "You can use your hands, sweetheart."

I unbuttoned the top button, then reached inside his boxer briefs, pulling out his hard cock. I'd seen it, felt it inside me, but holding it in my hand—I couldn't even wrap around it, soft and hard at the same time—it made my heart trip in my chest.

He was like that because of *me*. I'd done that to him. Me. Lucy Braverman. I knew I was hot—men told me that often —but I didn't know that the one man I'd always wanted, wanted *me.* It was fucking heady.

"You're so big," I murmured.

"Who are you comparing me to?" There was a warning in his voice. *Jealousy.* Delicious.

"No one," I said. "It's an objective truth. You're...big."

"Good," he said satisfied. "Spit in your hand."

I did.

"Stroke and squeeze. Not like—yeah, there you go. Get

me harder and thicker—I want to be so heavy in your mouth you aren't sure you can hold me."

I did what he demanded, stroking and squeezing, stroking and squeezing, watching, fascinated, as his cock got harder, thicker, almost pulsing as I touched it.

"There you go, now wrap your hands around my thighs and open that beautiful mouth. If I go too deep, if it's too much, squeeze my thighs and I'll take it easy on you. It's your first time, after all. Isn't it, sweetheart? Now, open. And keep those pretty eyes on me."

I opened my mouth, and a moment later the crown of his cock was between my lips. I took an exploratory lick, tasting smoke and musk and man. I shuddered and my pussy fluttered from the taste.

"A little more," he said, but stayed still, so I had no choice but to bob my head forward and capture more of him in my mouth.

"Suck on the crown."

I did, just like it was a lollipop, applying suction and working him deeper and deeper, licking and sucking and delighting in the way he tensed.

"Yes, that's right. That's a good girl. Keep going until you feel like you're about to gag. And watch those teeth."

Carefully, my mouth so wide it almost ached, I edged forward, wrapping my lips tighter. Experimenting with my tongue, his cock filling my mouth until it hit my soft palate, I gagged. I started to pull back, but he stopped me with a hand on my head.

"No, sweetheart. Stay there. You can breathe, you're fine. You're going to get used to having my cock in your mouth like this until you can take me deeper. In fact, I think this is what I'm going to do whenever you start causing trouble or saying shit I don't like. Plant my thick cock in your mouth and stay here until you settle down."

I should've hated the controlling nature of his words, but they tingled inside me. It was bonkers, but I wanted him to take me in hand that way. I wanted to be *handled*, with his big, rough, steady hands, the way he was holding my head now.

I inhaled through my nose, trying to manage the strangeness of something so warm, so hard, his scent so overpowering, filling my mouth and pushing against my throat. And, oddly, he was right, I began to settle and calm. Oh, I was wet, and my pussy was still fluttering, but I felt safer than I had in a long time.

Especially as he praised me in a low voice.

"Yeah, that's right. That's my good girl. Feels nice, doesn't it? Being controlled this way? Knowing you're in my hands, under my care? We're just going to stay like this for a while until I can't take it anymore. And while we do, I'm going to tell you a story. But first..."

He thrust his hips a tiny bit further forward, until his cock pushed against the top of my mouth, my throat, and I gagged again.

"Breathe through your nose," he instructed. "You're fine. You're safe, sweetheart. You can take me like this, I promise. You were *meant* to take me like this."

He was right. I calmed down immediately.

"Brave girl," he praised. "Sweet girl. I'm so proud of you. Now...where was I? Oh, yes."

And then he began.

19

"Once upon a time, there was a princess. She was lonely and ignored by the queen and king, and while she did everything she could to get their attention, they were too obsessed with their money, their status, and their hockey team to give her what she needed. The little girl told herself she was fine. She was independent; she didn't need anyone. And years later, when her parents died, it came true. A knight showed up in her life. He should've been her hero, he wasn't up to the task, so he banished her away to another kingdom for years. And though he regretted it every damn day of his life—though he hated himself for it—he told himself it was better this way, that she'd find friends and get a real education in another kingdom, with other, better people responsible for her safety and well-being."

Blake pulled slightly out of my mouth before pushing back in.

"Years went by, and the princess grew up into a queen. Until one day, she appeared back in the kingdom, tall and beautiful and proud, brave and strong as all hell, shocking the knight to his core, turning his whole life upside down, and making his guilt so bad he could barely sleep at night."

He tugged on my hair, pulling me closer. The story was too much, his cock was too much. I struggled to breathe and not grip his thighs to make him think I wanted to stop. I didn't want this to end. Not his cock in my mouth, not his story, not how close I felt to him.

Sighing in pleasure, he continued, weaving a spell around me in the quiet office.

"When he did sleep, he dreamed of all the ways he could defile the queen, all the ways he could make her his. Especially when she flaunted herself in front of other men. He told himself to stay away, until one day the queen ventured out into the world and gave herself to a man she did not belong to, because she belonged to the knight. At that moment, the knight's control snapped, because even though he knew he didn't deserve the beautiful queen, no other man did either. Instead, he claimed the queen, making her his...but early in the morning, as he watched her sleep, innocent and sweet—and yes, too good for him—he once again felt guilty for all the ways he let her down...so he left. He left her there, even though everything in his body made him wish he'd done otherwise, even though he thought of her in every waking moment and missed the feel of her with every single breath he took. And his cock? Oh, his cock missed her too. And his tongue? It missed her taste."

As he said the word "cock," I felt it expand in my mouth, somehow harder, thicker, more aggressive. And even though he didn't move, the girth of it threatened to choke me. My cheeks ached from the strain, my lips burned from the stretch, but when I tried to pull back again, he pulled my ponytail, keeping me in place with one dominant hand while the other tenderly stroked my cheek, quieting me.

So I stayed with his cock in my mouth like a pacifier, breathing through my nose as I continued to listen.

"He worried about her, too. He shouldn't have worried, though. For the queen appeared later that morning, flanked by her ladies in waiting, tall and strong and beautiful and brave as always, in no way cowed by the knight and his shitty, cowardly behavior. He hadn't diminished her spark one bit, and when other men were drawn to it, all he wanted to do was kill *each and every single one of them.*"

His hips shoved forward, almost like he wasn't in control of his movements, pushing against my throat, making me gag. I squeezed his thighs and he immediately retreated, but now his thumb stroked my lips where they wrapped around his cock.

"Now the queen had a potion she thought was magic, and was desperate enough to do something stupid by giving it to the knight, making him unknightly, making him lose so much control he could've hurt her. But what she didn't know was that the potion she held in her hand came nowhere close to the potion created between her perfect thighs, or the magic that existed inside her. The knight discovered her treachery, but because he was a bad man who did not deserve knighthood, he drank the potion anyway. Then when he did defile *her and her queenly mouth and royal cunt,* he wouldn't feel guilty."

The last sentence came out in a low, almost desperate moan.

"Lucy," he murmured.

"Hmm?" I tried to ask, the sound muffled by his cock.

"Oh, fuck, that felt so good," he said. "But what's going to feel better is if you tip your head back a bit and swallow and then open that pretty little throat for daddy's cock."

My eyes got wide, and I tried to shake my head.

"Squeeze my thighs if that's a no," he prompted.

I considered. It was scary, but the best things in life were. So far, all Blake had done was make me feel safe. This would be safe too. He'd take care of me. And since when had I avoided scary things?

So instead of squeezing his thighs, I stroked them.

His eyes shut.

"You perfect thing. You were made for me. Put your hand between your thighs and play with yourself. I can help you with this part."

I did what he said, unsurprised to discover wetness dripping down my thighs as I swirled my fingers around my clit and watched him. He lifted my chin, tilting my head back so my throat elongated. Straightening, opening.

"Deep breath in through your nose, sweetheart," he coaxed, and as I followed instruction, he slowly pushed closer and closer, until I felt his cock slide—oh shit, oh hell —into my throat. Deeper and deeper, until he had nowhere left to go and my nose was resting against the skin above his cock, surrounded by his smell. I swallowed, I had to swallow, and I was rewarded by a low, thick groan.

My hand started working faster between my thighs, because being held by him, trapped by him, surrounded by him, choked by him, by this man who I'd wanted before I knew what it meant to want someone...it was more than I could handle, and oh god oh god I needed to—

"No," he said sharply. "I know you're close, I can feel you moaning and whimpering around me, but you do *not* get to come."

"But please," I tried to beg, but his cock captured the words.

He shook his head. "As pretty as your eyes are while begging me right now, it's not time yet. Slow down and tease yourself. If you come, that will be the last time you do it for a whole fucking month."

That was a threat I didn't like, but I listened anyway and obeyed, gentling my touches and straining at my need.

He stroked my cheek again, easy and tender, like his cock wasn't shoved all the way down my throat.

How had he not come yet?

As if he'd heard me, he laughed.

"I do have some control over myself, you know. And your tight little throat feels too good to give up just yet. Now, start moving your fingers faster again, I want to see how many times you can edge yourself before you have to stop entirely."

I tried to shake my head, there was no way...

"Lucy, what did I say earlier? I'm in charge here. I'm taking care of you, I promise. But you have to trust me. And yourself. You're so brave and so strong. You can do this, sweetheart. Now, tight little circles around that clit. I want to feel you moan and whimper and beg around my cock as I force myself not to come...I'm edging myself too, you know."

He watched me, seeing everything. But in that moment, I saw him, too. Saw care and concern and affection that he'd hidden from me for so long, mixed in with the lust and desire. As I played, trying so hard to follow his orders, he pulled back and pushed forward again, sawing in and out of my throat, making me gurgle and gag as I fought to breathe, fought to not come, fought—

"Oh, fuck," he groaned, and as I watched, his pupils dilated. "There goes my control. You can come now, little troublemaker. Come while daddy fucks that throat and pours everything down inside you. Come while I make that mouth and throat and every part of you *mine*."

I moaned, my fingers working fast around my clit,

soaked and desperate. My eyes were fixed on his as he started powering into my throat, doing nothing more and nothing less than fucking my face. Every part of my body tightened, and then as he threw back his head and came with a roar, his cock choking me, I swallowed him down and came too, the word "mine" echoing in my head and my heart.

Finally, he started to soften and slipped out of my throat, my mouth, leaving me gasping on the floor, seeing stars. The intensity of the experience had overwhelmed me and tears streamed down my cheeks.

He stumbled a bit before righting himself, then scooped me off the floor and carried me to his desk chair. Setting me in his lap, he rubbed my back and murmured softly in my ear, calming me as I cried.

"Too much?" he asked.

I shook my head. "No."

He sighed, settling his chin on my head. "Good."

His cock, still hard, poked at my hip.

"You're—"

"It's still kicking in," he laughed. "Vice also works like Viagra. I'm giving you a second to recover before I wreck you all over again."

I rested against his chest, heart pounding, replaying that whole experience in my head as I tasted him on my tongue. He'd lied though, because he lifted me up moments later from his lap before dropping me down—right on top of his hard cock.

I screamed, quickly silenced by his hand on my mouth.

"Shh, none of that. We can't get caught, little troublemaker."

"But it's so much," I cried behind his hand.

"Recovery time's over, sweetheart," he said, pushing my

hips so I began to slide down his cock. From this angle, he was everywhere, and I felt so, so full. "I need to fuck you, hard and fast, and you're going to be a good girl and *take it,* aren't you?"

I whimpered, throat hurting from earlier.

He lifted his hand from my mouth.

"Lucy, I said, you're going to take it, aren't you? What do you say?"

I turned my head to look up at him, dredging up my last bit of energy to bat my lashes at him and say:

"Make me, daddy."

20

BLAKE

ake me, daddy.

Oh, I'd make her. If that's how she wanted to play it, we'd play it.

My body had never needed to fuck as badly as it did now, with her sweet wet cunt strangling my cock. Need pounded through me, and just like I'd told her, it didn't take me out of my mind, only honed my desires sharply to one sole focus—her.

"Lift your arms," I ordered, and she did. I pulled off her top, and out bounced her tits, naked and bare and perfect to play with.

To bite.

To suck.

To make her scream.

I went to town on them, treating my teeth to one and then the other, covering her mouth again with my hand in case someone heard her and we both got screwed. Her pussy clenched around my cock, pulsing in time with my bites, her cries blocked by my hand.

"Sweetheart, my cock is too busy right now to be an effective gag. Can you be quiet for daddy?"

Her eyes warmed and she nodded, holding in her sweet cries and keeping us both safe. That handled, I went back to worrying her nipples with my teeth and lips and tongue, sucking and biting, demanding without words that she come like this, from nothing but my cock in her cunt and my mouth ravaging her breasts.

She did, sucking my cock tight within her and drenching it as she tensed and then released. My cock strained, because I also needed to come again. Gripping her hips, not worrying about the bruises I knew I'd leave with my fingers, I lifted her up and slammed her back down on top of me, forgetting in my fervor that this was only her second time. I bounced her up and down on my cock until she got the rhythm, raising and lowering with me as quickly as she could, but not quick enough. I powered into her in my desk chair, aware of her soaking me and the leather with her juices, loving the idea that I'd smell her here even after she was gone.

No.

Not gone.

"You're not going *anywhere*," I told her, and she blinked, mumbling something against my hand.

I moved it.

She immediately tilted her head back to kiss me, which I avoided by twisting and biting her neck, trying to ignore the momentary flash of pain in her eyes, diffused by needy pleasure.

"I can't—really—" she gasped as she rose over me and slid back down, then up, "—go anywhere right now, so I think we're good."

She'd misunderstood me. I didn't mean right now when

I was fucking her, I meant after, when our release had dried. Later, someday, when she realized she didn't want to be tied down to a joyless man twice her age.

But I wasn't going to explain that, or get in an argument, not when my body was urging me on. Instead, I wrenched her down, covering her mouth again, taking over, pounding hard into her pussy as deep as I could get, spewing guttural nonsense as I did.

"That's right, troublemaker. You aren't going anywhere, are you? Can't get away, not with me holding you so tight. I can fuck you and fuck you and fuck you, and you won't escape, you'll just take it like a good girl. You want me to make you? Oh, I'll make you. Make you take every inch of me and every single drop of my cum in that warm, hot, tight, perfect pussy. And then I'll do it all over again. You're going to feel me for days."

She nodded eagerly so I continued, spine sparking, balls tightening, knowing I was about to come harder than I ever had in my entire life.

"You unleashed something inside me and I'm not going back. You're going to get me raw and hard and ready. You like that, don't you sweetheart? You're drenching my cock. Rub that little clit for me and come again."

Eyes glazed, she rushed to do what I said. I wasn't used to this version of Lucy, one who obeyed and didn't fight back. I liked it. Later, I wanted her to fight me. Later, I wanted her to struggle.

But for now, I liked her sweet and submissive this way. With a muffled moan, she tightened around me and came again.

I shut my own mouth to contain my shout of triumph, knowing that no one had ever seen her like this but me— and no one ever would.

The need to fuck deeper, harder, to make her hurt so good, overwhelmed me. I dragged her off my lap, even as my cock protested.

"What—" she was still coming.

"Over the desk with you."

Her legs almost buckled, so I stood, lifting and depositing her so she leaned over the desk and her bare ass faced me. Unable to stop myself, I ordered her to grab the desk and stay bent over before kneeling behind her and shoving my head between her legs, sucking her lower lips into my mouth and eating her pussy.

She couldn't contain her sounds and cried out. I just had to pray the walls were thick enough that no one would hear her, because I couldn't worry about that right now. Not when I could taste her, feast on her, force her over the edge again as she shook and writhed over me, squeezing her legs around my ears like the sexiest winter hat I'd ever had the pleasure of wearing.

Only when she started whining that it was too much did I relent, kissing her pussy and moving away to rise and stand behind her. The logical part of me loved that she'd been a virgin because it meant I could fuck her raw. The caveman part of me loved that she'd been a virgin, period. Both parts were gross assholes, but I didn't really give a shit. No, I just spread her legs wide, delivering smacks to her ass just because I felt like it, and then leaning over her and whispering in her ear,

"You ready for daddy to fill you up with his cum, troublemaker? I'm about to make a cream pie out of your pussy."

The sound that came out of her was unholy, and also the sexiest fucking sound I'd ever heard in my entire goddamn life.

Still.

"Say 'yes, daddy,'" I said. "Say yes, or I'll just edge you for a while."

She shook her head weakly.

I laughed. It sounded almost diabolical.

"Yes, daddy."

I could barely hear her, she was so hoarse from screaming my name and the way I'd worked her throat earlier. But the words did something to me. I didn't want responsibility for anyone, but for her...

For her I'd take on every task, commit to every ask, fulfill every request, just to see her goddamn smile.

I wanted to tell her that.

I wanted to kiss her.

I couldn't do either. It would take us down a dangerous path of intimacy and expectations that would lead nowhere but trouble, and she was enough trouble as it was.

Instead, I smacked her ass again.

"Poor sweetheart," I murmured. "Don't worry. Once I make a mess of your pussy, I'll take care of you. Hydrate you, clean you up, and then we'll start *all* over."

"Oh god." She groaned, and I couldn't tell if that was a good *oh god* or a bad one, but I was beyond caring by that point.

Not when I leaned back and looked at her pussy, red, swollen, raw, and begging for my cock.

So I gave it to her. No warm up, no preamble, just shoved right in and settled back into the home that was her pussy, tugging her head back by her hair, and went to fucking town. The slap of my hips against hers was the second best sound I'd ever heard, wet and almost echoing through the otherwise quiet room.

"One more," I demanded.

"I—"

I cut her off with an especially hard thrust. "Yes, you can. One more for me, little troublemaker."

To make sure it happened, I bent forward and bit down on her neck.

With a cry—the first best sound—she came, shuddering, cunt clenching and releasing around my cock. That's all it took, everything in me narrowing down to the feeling of where we connected, and I came, filling her full.

My life practically flashed in front of my eyes—my future, at least—and there she was, with me in all of it.

It scared the shit out of me even if it made me come harder than ever.

I wanted that.

Couldn't have it.

Didn't deserve to have it.

And once she figured that out, she'd move on.

But I was going to use her sweet body and luxuriate in her sweet scent and memorize every inch of her before that happened.

So when I was finished coming, I did exactly as I'd promised. Placed her on the desk gently as she trembled, soothing her, stroking her, finding water and lifting her head so she could slowly sip it, cleaned off her pussy with my suit jacket, and then...

...fucked her all over again.

And again.

And again.

21

LUCY

I'd never been to his house before.

I'd thought about it, pictured it, imagined what it would feel like to be invited there, even as I told myself it would never happen.

And finally, here I was.

I didn't even need to pinch myself to make sure it was real. My sore pussy was proof enough.

After Blake had wrecked me in his office, he'd bundled me up in his wet suit jacket. Making sure no one was around, he took me by the hand and led me to his car, picking me up and putting me in the front seat. He buckled me in, kissing me on the forehead.

"Gotta keep the most important thing safe," he murmured, creating a pang in my chest from the unexpected sweetness as he got in on the driver's side and started the car.

No one ever, in my entire life, had considered me the most important thing. I ruminated on it and what it could mean as he steered with one hand and grasped my hand with the other. He held it for the entire drive, and I let him, settling into his car the way I hoped I might be able to settle into his life.

Even though part of me knew better.

After all, we'd had sex again—several times—and he still hadn't kissed me.

Coach lived out in a beautiful cabin with big windows and tongue and groove ceilings in the woods of Gehenom, the town Tabb and Reina were located in. Even though his home was in the woods, he did have a neighbor—an old woman who happened to be outside on her porch when he lifted me out of the car.

"Who's with you, Blake?"

He stiffened. So did I, expecting him to drop me, distance himself, and make up an excuse. After all, what we were doing was entirely taboo, could get us both in trouble.

Instead he said, "Hi Maureen. This is Lucy. She's mine. I'd introduce you, but it's cold and she's tired, so I'm taking her inside the house."

She harumphed. "About time you brought someone home."

She's mine.

"Mine" had become my favorite word in the English language.

He didn't stop again as he opened the door and locked it behind him, still carrying me up the stairs, through a large, dark bedroom, and into a bathroom. I faded in and out as he put me in the hot shower, washed my body slowly and carefully, my body curved against his, taking special care to lather my hair and then rinse it out without getting shampoo in my eyes.

"No one's ever taken care of me like this before," I said sleepily.

There was a rough tone to his voice, one that I would've noticed more if I weren't completely wiped.

"No one, huh?"

But he let it go, working conditioner through my hair and rinsing that out, too, and then I was being lifted and carried out of the shower, dried off in a big, soft towel, and carried once again into a bedroom and placed in a big bed.

"Please don't leave me this time," I yawned. "Or I'll hate you."

"Lucy, you're in *my* house. I'm not leaving. I'm sleeping."

Getting into bed with me, he pulled me into his big, beautiful, safe, and strong arms. My back was to his front, nestling against him, I sighed.

"I could get used to this."

I never heard his response, because I was out like a light.

❤.❤

WHEN I WOKE UP, I WAS STILL IN HIS ARMS. AND HE WAS snoring.

I lifted my head to watch him, amused by how loud the snoring was. His eyes were closed, his face soft in the shadows of the dark night, his grip on me somehow tight, even as he slept. I considered basking in the feel of my body pressed to his, but I wasn't missing this opportunity to snoop. In so many ways, Coach was a closed book. I knew so little about his past, his family, what he wanted out of life beyond taking our team to the Frozen Four. Obviously I'd rather learn more from Blake himself, but for now, I'd take what I could get.

The memory of him avoiding my lips when I tried to kiss him hit me like a slap. I banished it. I'd get to the bottom of why he wouldn't kiss me, and once I learned it would start hurting. Not that it hurt now. I didn't care—

Stop lying to yourself, Lucy.

Okay. It fucking hurt. But what was I going to do, wake him up and demand answers? I mean, I *wanted* to, but I could piss him off and he could shut down on me...or worse, he could tell me something I didn't want to hear.

Ugh. Enough.

I carefully wriggled out of his hold. He groaned and flipped over onto his stomach, still snoring. My earlier inclination to keep snuggling with him had disappeared with my shitty thoughts. It was chilly in his bedroom, the air conditioning on way too high. I suddenly felt cold, too cold. I needed clothes, needed to cover my bare body. I went into his closet to find a shirt to put on, rummaging around until I found an old Gehenom Beasts jersey with Blake's last name and the number 18 stitched across the back.

I pulled it on over my head. Even with my height, it fit me like a dress, and I had to roll the sleeves up multiple times to make it even remotely wearable. I decided then and there I was keeping the jersey, even if I didn't get to keep the man.

Blow job tax and all that.

That decided, I roamed silently around the bedroom. There were no photos anywhere, no personal items. It was clean and sterile, lonely and sad. So I contented myself by imagining jazzing it up with pops of color here and there, throw pillows, my colorful dresses mixed in with his boring black suits and white starched shirts.

The more I snooped, the more I realized just how empty Blake's life was, how solemn, how—I wrinkled my nose— boring.

Well, that's why he had me.

Giving up on the bedroom, because there were no fun secrets, I continued into the hallway, opening and closing doors. They were all bedrooms, as meticulous and impersonal as his own. One room was set up as a gym, with mats, a weight bench, and a rowing machine. I lost a few minutes in there, picturing Blake all shirtless and sweaty, and let out a sigh.

Maybe we could put that rowing machine to good use...

Shaking myself out of that fun thought, I closed the door, and continued until I reached the last one, opening it.

Aha.

An office.

I entered, knowing it was more than a little shitty to snoop, but I didn't care—I had to learn more about him somehow.

Making my way around the desk, my brows drew together.

Because this room was not staid, or sterile, or boring, or impersonal—not at all.

The desk was covered in framed photos and notes, some of hockey plays, some of recaps on the team. It was the framed photos that stopped me in my tracks, though. Because they were of *me.*

Yearbook photos starting from when my parents died to when I graduated high school, lined up neatly in silver frames. My heart pounded in my chest, because this was... this was...

I didn't know *what* this was. Blake's story time earlier while I'd been sucking his cock had made it seem like he'd cared. But here it was, actual proof. Where had he even gotten those photos? I guess they could've sent them to him because he was my legal guardian and all.

Guardian. Like our safeword.

I winced.

"Why stay away for so long?" I asked the empty office. "If I mattered so much, why did you leave me?"

The office didn't answer.

I jerked open the top drawer, and paused, reaching in and pulling out a pair of familiar Barbie Pink underwear.

My underwear.

A million feelings rushed through me. Relief, because it wasn't a stalker after all. Worry, because actually, it was. Satisfaction, because I had enough power over him that he wanted my panties. Disgust at both him for doing something so filthy, so creepy, and at myself for *liking* it. There was something hot about him stashing my panties away as a sexy little memento.

And finally, there was anger, because there was no reason for Blake to be creeping around and stealing my panties when he could have just *asked for them* and I would have gladly handed them right over. I'd done that earlier tonight, hadn't I?

I rifled through the rest of the drawer, coming up with a folder labeled LUCY. It had my grades, every award, photos of boys I'd kissed, every boarding school I'd been kicked out of, including the time I'd been expelled for stealing the headmaster's keys to his Lamborghini and joyriding it around campus. There were also documents for all the times I'd been written up for causing havoc on campus at Tabb...and black and white photos of me.

Was that in my *dorm* room?

What. The. Actual. Fuck.

Where had he gotten these photos?

How much of a stalker was he?

Opening his laptop, I powered it up. The password prompt appeared, and I immediately typed in Lucy.

Nope.

Wait.

Troublemaker.

Immediately, the screen began to load.

"Oh, Coach, you should know better than to have such a simple password," I snorted. I scanned the desktop until I found what I was looking for: an application called Surveillance025. I knew about it, because my friends' fiancés all used it to spy on them and "keep them safe."

I clicked on it and my heart turned into stone, like in a fairytale—one of the sad ones. It was both what I'd expected and dreaded, because it was video of my empty dorm room.

He'd been watching.

There were multiple screens with multiple cameras. Not one, but two, were aimed toward my bed.

My bed, where I'd gotten off the day my panties had gone missing.

I took a deep breath, trying to recalibrate, to rationalize. Because yeah, there was a dark, sick part of me that thought his obsession was kind of hot. I wasn't going to pretend it wasn't. But the other part of me *hated* this. Hated that he'd skulked around to watch me without my goddamn permission when he could've just talked to me, like the grown man he pretended to be. He'd made me feel like I was alone in my obsession, when he was clearly in as deep as I was.

No wonder he'd been able to find me at the hotel. How long had he been watching me? I felt terrified and claustrophobic, but mostly angry at the lies and the secrets.

What else was Blake Samson hiding from me?

I wanted to storm into the bedroom, to scream at him, to throw things, beat him with my fists, but something he'd said to me earlier rang in my head, the "lock her up in a tower" bit.

Is that what he'd do to me if he found out I'd caught him?

Or worse, would he feel guilty and awful and retreat again, leaving me out in the cold?

I needed to think.

I needed to not be here.

I headed downstairs and located my purse in the front hallway, grabbing my phone to text Leslie.

> Can you come get me? Like now?

Lucy, it's the middle of the night. Leslie's asleep.

Shit. That must be Mason.

> Please, it's important.

Fine, I'm on my way. Where are you?

> Coach's house.

Ellipses appeared and disappeared. Mason clearly had no idea how to respond to the revelation that his fiancée's best friend was at his coach's house in the middle of the night, obviously up to no good.

Finally, he responded.

I'll send someone.

Shit.

Someone else was bad. Someone else could talk. This still needed to be a secret.

> No, Mason, it has to be you.

More ellipses, before he replied.

> Don't worry. I'll send Emory. He'll keep your
> secret.

I relaxed, slightly. I knew enough of Emory's secrets for him to keep mine, too. I hoped.

Before I left, I scribbled a note to Blake. A continuation of the story when he'd had me backed in a corner and trapped around his cock. My weak, exhausted pussy clenched at the thought, making me even angrier.

Mine, he'd called me.

We'd finally gotten somewhere. I finally had someone I belonged to, or at least I thought I did. By being a fucking unthinking idiot, he was taking that away from me, too.

I put my pink panties on top of the note, just in case I wasn't clear enough. And with that, I headed outside to wait for Emory and get the hell out of here before I stormed back inside, up the stairs, and unleashed my fury and rage and hurt on the man sleeping there.

Minutes later, Emory pulled up in his McLaren. He glanced over at me when I got in the car.

"If I ask what happened, will you hit me?"

I turned my head to glare at him.

"No, but I'll tell that lit professor of yours what you've been up to."

He sighed. "No, you won't. Your bark is worse than your bite, Lucy."

He was right. Maybe if it were the other way around, I'd protect myself better from being hurt by Blake.

"If I ask if you're okay, will you threaten me again?"

I shut my eyes, unwilling to let him see the truth.

"I'm fine."

For a moment, he was quiet as we drove, the woods around town turning into streetlights, sidewalks, and bars. A few drunk students stumbled around, laughing, but otherwise off-campus was quiet.

"My bite *is* worse than my bark," he told me. "And even though my professor may not know it, I refuse to give up on her. I won't let my own personal demons get in the way of our endgame."

I shook my head, still refusing to open my eyes, or he'd see how glassy and wet they were. I refused to show anyone else my pain.

"That's nice for you, but you don't know what it's like to be rejected your whole life. I've had enough of it. I won't take more. I can't force Coach to do what he doesn't want to do, so protecting myself is the next best thing."

"You might be surprised," Emory murmured, but didn't elaborate more.

He was quiet as we drove the rest of the way to my dorm, but he did put on Sabrina Carpenter for me, making me soften a little. Especially when he said, "If you want, you can crash with Matt and me. Might take you out of the line of fire, and I know I wouldn't want to be alone right now."

I softened even more, grateful to have people in my life who cared, even if the one person I wished cared enough didn't.

The most important thing, Blake had called me.

Now it felt like a lie.

"Thanks for being a good friend and not spilling my secrets," I told Emory.

"Thanks for being a good friend and not spilling mine," he replied.

22

BLAKE

I woke up reaching for her, only to feel a warm, empty pillow beside me.

"Lucy? Come back to bed," I called, yawning. It must have been early in the morning. The sun hadn't risen yet, and all I wanted to do was curl Lucy up in my arms and go back to sleep for another couple of hours.

Except there was no response.

"Lucy? Troublemaker?"

Nothing.

Rolling out of bed, I grabbed a pair of sweatpants and searched the bathroom. She wasn't there. The other bedrooms. Still no. My heart began to thump, faster and faster, as I called for her and searched for her, dread percolating in my stomach.

I knew before I knew.

The door to my office was open. Just a crack, but still open.

She wasn't in there, and it looked undisturbed, but she must have seen. The photos, the dossier, everything.

Running down the stairs, I grabbed my keys with no real plan in place. Just panic. Then I saw it.

A note on the kitchen counter, covered by her panties— the ones I'd stolen.

I picked up her panties and placed them back in my pocket, as if by keeping them safe, I could reverse this whole hellish experience and she'd appear in my kitchen and say "just joking."

But the note made it clear that wasn't happening.

The queen never wanted to be locked away in a tower, especially not from a lying knight who watched her from the shadows but refused to be in the light with her. She wanted him, but she wanted an honest kingdom more.

So she left.

And she lived happily ever after.

Alone.

Unless you come clean and explain everything, asshole.

I stared down at the note. Her anger was clear in every word, but that wasn't what had frozen me in the kitchen. I could barely keep from falling to my knees and roaring in anguish. I'd hurt her. Badly. So badly, she'd left without waking me. Obviously she'd discovered the photos and the dossier on her along with her panties. I should've come clean to her before, but would she even have listened? Understood something I didn't fully understand myself?

It didn't matter right now. All that mattered was that she was okay. Was safe somewhere. I ran back up the stairs to my office, not even bothering to sit down at my desk as I checked the cameras. She wasn't in her dorm. I ran back downstairs to check my phone. The GPS app showed her at an unfamiliar address—and when I searched it, no name came up.

Where the fuck had she gone? Where was she? Who was she with?

"Lucy, where the fuck are you? Come home," I said into the empty kitchen, barely aware what I was saying, or that I thought of it as her home too, now.

I called her phone multiple times. She didn't pick up. Each time, I grew more worried, and with that, angry— and then angrier. Yes, it was my fault that she'd left. But to sneak out on me was childish. To ignore me, even more so. She had to know how worried I was, how the terror was an endless punch to the gut. How the fuck could she do this?

Are you angry with her, or yourself? that jackass of an inner voice asked calmly.

I ignored the fucker and texted her.

> Please tell me you at least got home safely after you snuck out of my house like a bad dream.

She replied immediately.

> are u calling me a nightmare?

Of course I wasn't. She had to know I wasn't.

> The nightmare was waking up and not knowing where you were, or if you were safe.

didn't u think to check your cameras to see
where I was

Well, she had me there.

... ...

I did. And you weren't there.

that's because I went to emorys

The entire kitchen turned red. Redder still, as I fantasized driving over to Emory's and stabbing him to death
before fucking Lucy on top of his still-bleeding corpse.

I forced myself to slow my breathing, tossing my keys
across the kitchen before I could act on my worst impulses.
I'd hurt her, and so she'd acted out. I was still pissed at her
for that, but at least she was safe. And as angry as Emory
made me, I knew the kid wouldn't hurt her.

So you're safe.

Okay.

That's it? No explanation or apology?

You want an explanation? An apology? You
can have both when you come back. But I'm
not doing this over text like I'm one of your
friends.

Ellipses appeared and disappeared on the screen. Even
though I hoped it was because she was considering coming
back, facing me, and talking this out, I knew Lucy too well

for that. She was probably coming up with the most cutting retort possible.

I was wrong. It was worse.

Why won't you kiss me?

Fuck.

Fuck. Fuck. Fuck.

I swallowed painfully. It felt like I'd swallowed the blade of a hockey skate.

I couldn't tell her that, especially not over text. I could barely talk about it at all. How could I explain the way my foster father had fucked with my head? How undeserving I felt, of kissing, and what it would mean? It was a level of intimacy I wasn't worthy of. Kissing felt like responsibility, like care, like making a statement.

Kissing felt like love.

And love wasn't for me.

I stared at my phone, trying to come up with a response. All I had was:

Lucy...

We'll talk about it after the game, I promise. Just don't do anything stupid or that we'll regret, please.

More appearing and disappearing ellipses, and then came the cutting retort I'd expected.

I'm not the stupid one in this conversation.

She was right.

I threw my phone against the wall. It hit the backsplash and shattered in pieces into the sink.

Here I was, the violent man I'd always been afraid I'd become. I didn't deserve her. Wasn't worthy of her kisses, or otherwise.

Sinking to my knees, I shoved my hands through my hair. Short of driving over to Emory's, resisting killing him, and dragging Lucy back here, I wasn't sure what to do. Maybe she deserved a little space, until I could man the fuck up and explain to her what was wrong with me. And fucking fix it.

First, I needed to drag myself out of this hole I'd buried myself in.

23

I'm not the stupid one in this conversation.

I sat and stared at my unanswered text as Leslie gracefully flitted around me, getting ready for the game. I sat on her bed, sullen and sulking, not interested in seeing a man who hadn't shown one ounce of remorse. Even if it technically was my job to be there.

"But I don't want to go to the game," I whined as Leslie dragged me through the doors into the melee.

It wasn't that I didn't want to go to the game. It was that I didn't want to see Blake. He'd left me on read. And since I had no interest in being watched by the douchebag asshole creep who couldn't even get his dick out of his own ass long enough to reply to a *text*, I was hiding out in Leslie's old dorm room to avoid the cameras he'd planted.

"Yes, you do," she said. "It's the semi-finals. Besides, you wouldn't have put this much effort into how you looked if you didn't want to be seen."

"I *always* put effort into how I look," I pointed out. It was one of the few lessons my mother had taught me that I actually internalized.

"Seen by Coach," she clarified.

She was right.

I was pissed off and disappointed, but I wanted answers from him. And what's more, I wanted to see him. My body was getting used to the feeling of being held by him, and the absence of his chest against my back made me feel raw and like something was missing—something essential. I hated that I felt that way, but I did. I needed answers, I needed him to finally fucking kiss me. I needed *him*. That was the embarrassing truth:

I, Lucy Braverman, the woman who needed no one, needed Blake Samson.

Fuck.

I swallowed back tears that had this obnoxious way of showing up all the time.

I managed to keep them at bay on the way out of their apartment and in the car ride over to the arena. But after we parked and headed inside, I froze.

"I really don't want to do this," I said.

"Maybe, but you still can. Be brave, Braverman," Leslie said.

I glanced at her, distracted momentarily from my angst.

"How long have you wanted to use that?" I asked.

"Since I first learned your last name," she confessed.

Out of the blue, I hugged her. "Be my bestie forever, okay?"

She hugged me right back. "Okay."

I released her and she grabbed my hand, guiding me through the crowd of excited fans and into the stands. There was a more or less permanent spot for her—well, us—in the rows above the penalty box. We sat, Leslie blushing and excited in Mason's number. I had recklessly decided to wear Emory's number. I knew men who played (and coached) hockey. I knew how they felt when the woman they cared about wore another man's name and number on her back. If Blake actually cared about me, if he felt territorial toward me at all, I was playing with fire.

But since I wanted to set some things on fire right now, namely him, I was fine with it.

Like she'd followed my train of thought, Leslie shook her head.

"You're about to get your ass in so much trouble," she sang out, but then Mason waved at her and blew her a kiss, and she forgot all about me.

Emory, who was currently stretching, paused and looked at me, clearly alarmed.

What the hell are you doing, he mouthed.

I shrugged.

Making trouble, I mouthed back, winking.

He shook his head, and my gaze went where I knew it would: to the man in the suit, tablet in hand, conferring with Trey over a play or something. As if he could feel me staring at him, he turned his head, catching my gaze.

A small smile played on his lips, and he played with his tie...only for his lips to flatten into a grim line as he realized what I was wearing.

And then, because I felt like pissing him off, I stretched and turned around so he could see Emory's last name (van der Linde), and number (96) from all the best angles. It helped that I was wearing booty shorts and had curled my hair that morning. I could feel his perusal, and what's more, I could feel his barely banked anger as he stared at me.

Turning back around, I blew him a kiss and winked for good measure before taking my seat.

Blake slammed his hand on his tablet and blew his whistle, jerking his thumb at Emory and saying something. I strained my ears, but I couldn't hear over the loud chatter in the stands.

Emory looked pissed, but he pulled his helmet off his head and went back to the bench.

"Is he taking him out of the game?" Leslie whispered, eyes wide.

Oh shit.

What had I done?

Then Blake jerked his thumb at *me.*

I shook my head once.

No, I mouthed.

He jerked his thumb again.

People were watching the whole exchange, and some craned their necks to see who the highest-ranked hockey coach in the NCAA was talking to. When they saw it was me, the chattering and whispers got worse.

I didn't get embarrassed easily, I didn't. But having hundreds, maybe thousands, of people paying attention to me—especially when my face showed up on the jumbotron—was no match for my normal ability to shake things off.

Annoyed, I picked up my bag and told a wide-eyed Leslie, "See you later, if I live," before I was clunking down the metal stairs of the stands. I could feel the crowd's eyes on me as I climbed over the metal railing to get behind the bench. It would have been more elegant of me to have left the stands and used the player entrance, but fuck that. If Coach wanted to embarrass me, I'd embarrass him right back.

Coach, who currently stood in front of the bench, one foot on the boards, watched me instead of his players stretching.

When he saw me awkwardly making my way in, all Blake said was, "You work for the team, remember?"

Oh. Right.

This wasn't about me, this was about my *job*.

Still.

"Why are you benching Emory? He's first line," I challenged.

"Because he fucked around, and now he's going to find out. Want me to do the same to you?"

I could tell him *all about* fucking around and finding out. And from the tenseness of his jaw, he knew I could. But instead, he just pointed.

"Go refill everyone's water bottles and get towels. I want you standing there—" he pointed next to where he and Trey stood— "throughout the entire game in case we need you."

I opened my mouth. He was the stalker, how was I in trouble?

As if he read my mind, he said. "I'm your boss now, remember?"

Oh, and I could ruin that for him.

I could ruin everything for him. One sentence to the dean, and I could destroy his entire career—and my own future. That was the real fire I was playing with.

But I also remembered the way he'd carried me inside his house last night, carefully washing my body and making sure shampoo didn't get in my eyes, and I couldn't—wouldn't—do it.

So instead, I trudged off to refill water bottles and get towels like the good girl I sometimes pretended to be, even if I daydreamed about putting laxatives in his water bottle. That would've been a better choice than Vice. That's what he deserved.

As I headed to the tunnel, Emory called after me, "Don't cause any more trouble, troublemaker." He sounded huffy.

But not nearly as pissed as Coach when he turned to him and said, "Don't you fucking call her that, or I'll kick you off this team for good."

Emory slunk down where he sat. "Got it."

"Good."

Oh god. We were going to be spending a lot of time in close quarters for the next few hours, and I hoped we all survived.

♥‸♥

AFTER THE FIRST PERIOD, THE TEAM HEADED BACK TO THE locker room. I followed, sandwiched by Blake and Trey. I was careful not to even look at Emory, in case Coach saw me and decided to bench him for the rest of the season to teach him a lesson or to follow through on his earlier threat and kick him off the team entirely.

When we reached the locker room, Coach grabbed my upper arm, holding me back.

Trey looked over at him with questioning eyes.

"I need to talk to Lucy for a second. I'll be right in."

Trey's lips pursed, but he just shrugged and left us alone in the hallway.

"Lucy..." Blake trailed off, for once at a loss for words.

"Oh, I can help with this," I said. "Lucy, I'm sorry. Lucy, I fucked up. Lucy, I promise not to do sketchy shit anymore instead of talking to you directly about my feelings..."

His forest green eyes were paler than usual. He shut them, and swallowed, then reopened them, focusing on my face.

He spoke. "Lucy, what I did was wrong. I never in a million years should have bugged your dorm room, stolen your underwear, or hidden in your room and listened to you come—"

"Wait, I'm sorry. You did *what the fuck* now?" I interrupted.

He'd been in there when I'd jilled off? Oh god, I'd been fantasizing about him. I'd said his *name*. I was embarrassed, and I hated that. He was the one who should be embarrassed.

"No wonder you knew I was into you," I said. "That's so fucked up."

He nodded. "I know. It was. It is. I was in the middle of bugging your room when you showed up, and so I had to hide under the bed—"

"You fit under my bed? You're a giant!"

That didn't actually matter, but it was what occurred to me in the moment.

He clearly thought the same. "That's what you care about?"

"No, but I'm trying to picture it. You, underneath my bed while I was getting myself off..." I trailed off, really picturing it. "Did you wrap a hand around that big cock when you listened to me?"

His Adam's apple worked. "Are you trying to seduce me, or do you want an explanation? Because the former can't happen here, and the latter is more important right now, anyway."

Damn it, he was right. I was distracted by him too easily.

"It depends on how good the explanation is," I said honestly. "And you still haven't apologized."

He sighed, looking properly chastised. "You're right. I'm sorry, Lucy. I told myself I was bugging your room because I didn't trust that you wouldn't do something even more reck-less than usual, and wanted to make sure you were safe and stayed that way. I can't explain to you how essential it is to me that you're safe, but I need it like I need to breathe." He shook his head. "But that wasn't the only reason. I did it because I'm obsessed with you, because I can't stop thinking about you, because all I think about *is* you, and because the possibility of one of my players getting their sweaty hands all over you makes me want to knock their teeth out with a puck—or three."

Oh.

Oh.

"Obsessed?" I asked, my voice a little breathy.

He nodded solemnly, reaching out to tuck a piece of hair behind my ear.

"Completely obsessed."

"And you couldn't just...come to me and tell me this? You had to be all sketchy and secretive and do weird shit like steal my underwear?"

His eyes darkened, and he moved in closer, looming over me as he lowered his voice. "Do you really think that was weird? Because I think, secretly, you like it."

I swallowed. I wasn't going to lie.

"I did." I cleared my throat. "So what does this mean, for us?"

He hesitated. "It means that even if I wanted to stay away, I couldn't."

"I mean," I shrugged, smiling through the vulnerability. "Same."

"And I don't want any of these fuckers around you. I swear, Lucy. You wear someone else's jersey to a game again, and I won't bench him—I'll kill him."

"You don't have to worry about that," I told him. "Besides, I stole your jersey, and I'd rather wear that."

"Damn, I want to see that," he growled. His eyes cleared. "But you can only wear it—"

"In private, I know," I said. I wasn't going to risk his job or my future. "No one can find out about this. But if you kill anyone who gets near me, it goes the same for you. I need to know you won't be with anyone else." I swallowed, the next part hard to say out loud. But I would, anyway. "And I need to know why you won't kiss me."

Blake opened his mouth, but before he could answer, the door to the locker room opened, and Trey stuck his head out, looking annoyed.

"Coach, the team is waiting for you. I think whatever you need to talk about with your *ward* and our *assistant* can wait. Can't it?"

Coach nodded. He looked at me, eyes apologetic. But Trey cleared his throat and Coach turned away, walking past him into the locker room. Before the door shut, Trey looked at me.

"Whatever you're doing to him, stop."

"I'm not doing any—"

But the door banged shut on my denial, leaving me wondering what this meant for Blake and me, and more importantly, where things stood with him and other women.

I should've worried more.

♥♠♥

We were down by two points when it happened.

It was four minutes into the second period, and I was sandwiched between Blake and Trey behind the players' bench. I felt almost claustrophobic. Blake was pressed against me on one side, and Trey tried not to touch me on the other. In front of us sat fifteen players, focused on the game but still aware of my every move. I leaned back against the glass that separated the fans from the team, desperate to cool down from the heat radiating off of Blake's body, and did my best to focus on the game.

Taking Emory out had been a real mistake. The team was lagging, missing passes; our defense was uncoordinated and giving up two-on-ones; our goalie couldn't get in the zone, making it easy for the opposing team's center to score back to back with what seemed like half-assed attempts at a save.

Mason looked pissed but stole the puck and skated towards the net on a breakaway when the other team's defense dove in front of him, attempting to block the shot and dislodging the net in the process. The other team's defense said something that set him off, because he shoved them back, ripping off his gloves. The team was a mess. Emory was the glue that held them together, and without him they were a bunch of lone wolves instead of a pack.

The ref blew his whistle. Blake pointed at the ref and called him over. He and Trey argued with him emphatically, Trey's arms waving every which way. Blake leaned over the bench, sticking his face in the ref's and using his size and stature to intimidate him.

It must have worked, because the ref blew his whistle again, made the call, and the players lined up while Mason took his penalty shot.

Coach and Trey had their heads together as they made their way back to me, I strained to hear what they were saying.

"You know, my sister's here tonight."

"That's nice."

"No, she's here to see you."

"Why?"

"You invited her."

You could've heard my heart thud to the floor. Professor Putrovksi was here. Not only was she here, she was here for Blake. Blake, who was mine. Blake, who'd told me if another man got near me, he'd kill him, but hadn't had the chance to acknowledge it worked the same for him and other women. Hadn't had the chance, or had he avoided telling me it *wasn't* the same for him and other women? Did he know that she was my professor? Did he know about the potential intercollegiate program I was up for? Was there any chance I could have him and my dream?

Somehow everyone else missed my heart thud, too focused on Mason as he shot the puck straight past the other team's goalie into the net. It was an easy shot, changing our score from 0-2 to 1-2.

As the horn blared, the crowd roared, and Mason skated past the bench, high fiving his teammates as he tapped the goalie's pads. Coach made it back to where I waited.

The second he arrived I hissed in his ear, "You invited Trey's sister to the game?"

He rubbed his head. "Apparently."

"Who the fuck is she to you?"

He rubbed his head. "We need to talk about this later, Lucy."

"You know she's my professor, right?"

He blinked, shocked.

"Ah, fuck."

"Yeah," I hissed as Trey made his way back to us. "Fuck."

Blake raised his voice as Trey sat down. "Lucy, I need you to focus, and I need to focus. In order for us to do that, I need you to not get into trouble so I don't get distracted. Got it?"

What I got was that he was being a bossy asshole in public to make it seem like nothing was happening between us. I liked when he was a bossy asshole—but only in private. This made my ears steam.

"Will you let Emory play?"

He scowled. "No."

"Do you want me to do a strip tease on the ice during intermission?" I threatened.

He knew I would.

"Goddamnit." He turned to the box behind him, raising his voice. "Van der Linde, you're back in."

His replacement got off the ice. Looking grateful, Emory pulled on his helmet, jumped the barrier, and skated out onto the rink, tagging the backup winger out. He looked up in the stands for a moment at someone before shaking his head and taking his position on the ice.

Play resumed, and I sat between two grown men, aware that both their eyes were on me—for different reasons.

"I'm still pissed at you," I murmured to Blake.

A small, regretful smile played on his lips.

"I know."

"Fuck," Trey muttered.

I looked over at him. "What?"

"You're trouble, you know that?"

I did.

"You don't call her that," Blake snapped before he could stop himself.

"A fuck ton of trouble," Trey repeated.

This time, I smiled.

He was right. I was.

24

LUCY

With Emory back in the game, we quickly tied the opposing team's score and then surpassed it. The game ended, 4-3. But even though the fans and the team were in celebratory mode, I wasn't.

Because there was a woman here. To see Coach.

My professor. To see *my* Coach.

And he had fucking invited her.

Stalked *me*. Stolen *my* panties. Fucked *me* until I couldn't see straight. But invited *her*.

He and the team had disappeared into the locker room. I'd tried to follow, but he'd put an arm out and stopped me.

"I don't need you seeing college dick," he'd muttered, and anyone who overheard would have probably assumed that he was being protective, not territorial.

Well, except for Trey, who watched the entire exchange, eyes working. I narrowed my own eyes at him; he was trying to ruin everything I wanted with his stupid, age-appropriate sister.

I leaned against the wall outside the locker room, waiting. I still wasn't sure what I wanted to say or do. Coach had a lot to answer for, and I wasn't sure where we went from here. Had he really invited her? He'd seemed surprised when Trey had said something, but even Professor Putrovski had verified that there was something going on between them. Was I being played? Was I a current or future side piece?

Oh no. No no no. No the fucking hell no. No way. I'd put up with that shit like I'd put up with someone abusing an animal, which was not at all.

"Oh. Hi, Lucy."

Professor Putrovksi looked pretty in her high heels and cropped boyfriend jeans. She was perfectly put together, a little conservatively dressed, but her cleavage peeked out of her blue button down, making her neutral look sexy.

She looked nothing like me. She looked like an *adult*.

"Hi Professor," I trilled, resisting the urge to cross my arms, block the door, or maybe even rip the hair out of her scalp for daring to try to take what was so obviously mine.

But was he? He won't even let you wear his jersey in public.

"I didn't expect to see you here," she said, confused and a little wary. I must have been broadcasting my feelings about her appearance loudly—too loudly.

"Oh, I assist the team, so they keep me around," I said easily.

She visibly relaxed, and I reminded myself that this was the person who could change the entire trajectory of my career—even if being with Blake could change the entire trajectory of my life.

I was stuck. What did I do? Did it even matter? This clearly wasn't up to me.

"Oh, that makes sense. I was supposed to meet my brother and Coach Samson here after the game. Are they still in the locker room?"

Go away.

I forced myself to smile. "Post-game talk," I said. "They should be out later, but it could be awhile. The press will probably do interviews, plus they have to talk to the players...if you want, I can take a message for him."

A message for him. Like I was his secretary.

At "could be a while," her back straightened.

"I think I'm fine waiting here," she told me, and even though she forced a smile, the hostility coming off me was not the kind of thing you could ignore.

And she wasn't going to. "Lucy, are you sure assisting the team is a good use of your time? You should be studying. That's what's important, isn't it? If you want, I can talk to Coach Samson for you about it at dinner tonight."

Dinner.

They were having *dinner*.

I knew a date included some sort of food or beverage, but that meant they'd planned it, that Coach had made a reservation somewhere. He'd known and he hadn't told me. He let me just stand there like a fool and tell him I'd kill whatever woman he spent time with...what was he playing at?

Then, clearly feeling awkward, she offered, "Maybe you and Trey can come with? Not as a double-date thing, of course, but you're both family, and it's good to get to know each other's families early, in my opinion..."

Excuse me?

Was she inviting me on their date?

Did she think they'd get serious enough that including families was important? And since when was I even Blake's family?

I didn't answer her.

She sighed. "Lucy, did I do something?"

Oh, fuck. I forced my face to look friendly.

I leaned in and lowered my voice. "I was hesitant to tell you this earlier, but the thing is...the reason Blake is single is that he doesn't date. Ever."

I had no idea if I was lying or not. For all I knew, Blake went on dates six nights a week and twice on Sundays, although the thought of him being with anyone else gave me figurative hives.

She absorbed this, and from the way her eyebrows raised, it was very obvious she did *not* believe me.

"And why would you be privy to that information?"

"Because," I said, knowing it could get me in all sorts of shit and not caring whatsoever. "I'm his."

"His..." she trailed off.

I should've finished that sentence, let him off the hook, but I shrugged and refused to qualify it. My professor's eyes narrowed as they swept my whole body, analyzing me as more than her student. I read her face as she considered if I was a potential threat before decidedly dismissing me.

"His..." she filled in the blank. "His kid, right."

"He never adopted me," I said immediately. I was no kid, least of all Blake's. I couldn't tell if she was purposefully trying to antagonize me or honestly misunderstanding me, but either way, I didn't like it.

"Oh? But he is your legal guardian, yes? He's responsible for you?" A wry, not particularly kind smile lit her face. "You know, Lucy, it's normal to feel...territorial over a parental figure. But at some point, you need to let them be happy."

I should've kept my mouth shut, but then I'd never been good at keeping my mouth shut.

"Oh, I'm very good at *making* him happy," I said.

Her eyes widened, but before she could respond, the door burst open, and Blake stood there in all his glory.

God, he was beautiful. He'd been inside me so recently, and all I wanted was to wrap myself around him, plant a kiss on his lips, and make it clear who he belonged to.

But did he? He'd called me his, but never said he was mine.

"Blake," the professor said with a happy trill to her voice, her earlier low, suspicious tone forgotten.

Coach glanced at her. "No interviews tonight," he said shortly. "Lucy—"

Ha. Satisfaction filled me at his response. He didn't know who she was.

Trey pushed his way out. "Hey, sis," he said.

He gave her a warm hug, then, holding her arm, turned to Coach. "Remember my sister Alison? And your date?"

"My—" Blake's eyes looked blank, and then recognition snapped in them. "Oh, Alison. Right! Our...date. Tonight."

The confirmation was a slap in the face, the kind that left a mark.

The professor—Alison—straightened her shoulders, tossing her hair. It was a poor imitation of my own hair toss, but then I doubted she'd practiced in the mirror for days until she got it right.

"Yes, our date. It's late, you must be starving. Good game, by the way. You really pulled it off in the second half."

Second *half*? Did she even know anything about hockey? I mean, for the daughter of an NHL team owner, I didn't know as much as I should, but even I understood hockey had three periods. How the hell could Blake even consider going on a date with someone who, sure, was brilliant when she taught animal behavior, but was an idiot otherwise?

Blake looked at me over her head, and for a moment I thought he was going to refuse, to tell her he had plans.

Please refuse.

But then Trey said, almost sharply, "Coach, you don't want to miss your reservation. It's not like you to bow out on commitments."

There was a deeper meaning to his words, and Coach forced a smile to his face that didn't reach his eyes. Still, he didn't speak.

"I was just talking to Lucy here," Alison added. "She's welcome to join us. After all, she's one of my students...did she tell you?"

Coach nodded slowly. "Yes, she told me."

"Oh, good." Alison looked lost for a moment but quickly recovered. "In fact, she's up for a special intercollegiate pre-vet program, and as long as her grades, activities, reputation, and *recommendation letters* are up to par, she's a shoo-in." Alison stressed recommendation letters, and her point was clear.

Don't fall for it, don't fall for it, I begged Coach with my eyes. But I could tell she'd caught him with "recommendation letter." He knew what she was implying, and he wasn't going to risk messing with my future—even if it meant he wouldn't be in it, because he was a fucking martyr and a jackass.

"Yeah, we shouldn't miss our reservation," he said. "And I'd rather spend some alone time with you, if that's alright."

That was all I needed to hear.

I turned to go, even though I could feel his eyes burning a hole in my straight, stiff back.

I didn't need this shit.

Didn't need any of it.

Especially when I had his car keys.

I had no interest in being overlooked, forgotten, and uncared for ever again. Clearly Blake had just wanted some young virgin pussy and had no deeper interest in me. The photos made no sense, but...neither did him going on a date with someone else *right after* he'd fucked me. I didn't care if we had to keep things secret, or that he was protecting me—he could have canceled, made up an excuse, *something*.

Still, as I reached the end of the hallway, I turned to look, just to see if he really was watching, but his eyes were on Alison...

...and her hand was on his chest as she laughed at something he said.

This time, I didn't even try to swallow down the tears, letting them blur my vision as I headed out of the arena, out of their sight...and out of his life.

Time to make my own.

25

BLAKE

I t took me five minutes to get rid of her.

But it was five minutes too long.

"You know," I said, shifting away from Trey's sister's hands on me—hands that felt like claws. I only wanted one woman's hands on my chest, and it wasn't hers. "I'm tired. Can we raincheck?"

Her lips pursed, and I heard Trey cough nearby. I'd already forgotten her name, but I wanted to be far fucking away from her. Lucy's retreating back had called to me, and I could tell how upset she was by the stiff way she'd held herself as she'd walked away from us—from me. I needed to go to her, to explain, to...something.

I didn't know how to explain anything, other than with my cock. What could I give to the little troublemaker that she deserved? Maybe this was when she figured out that I wasn't worthy of her, was too old, too solemn and boring and pissed off all the time. Maybe she'd be grateful I hadn't kissed her, because she could share that with someone she belonged with.

No. Every bone, every sinew, every cell in my goddamned

body rejected the idea of letting her be with anyone else. Because I'd realized something, watching Lucy disappear down the hallway. I hated watching her walk away from me. I hated the idea of letting her leave. Because in a short period of time, this girl, this *woman*, had not only gotten under my skin, but burrowed her way deep into my heart and made a home there.

I loved her.

Fuck.

I loved Lucy Braverman.

And I was going to go to hell for it.

First, though, I had to get rid of Trey's sister. Truthfully, I had no memory of setting up a date with her. But then again , I'd been so focused on Lucy that everything else in my life had taken a backseat, and rightly so.

Unaware of my internal turmoil, the woman opened her mouth, then shut it.

"I'm so sorry, Abby," I apologized.

"Alison," she snapped. "You know, Blake, I'd heard good things about you from my brother. That you were a noble, confident man, the kind who knew what he wanted and what's more, did the right thing. Not the kind of man who lusts after a girl half his age because she's got perky boobs and wears ass-bearing shorts." She glanced at her brother. "You lied."

Ah, fuck.

Fuck, fuck, fuck.

She'd digested me, read me right, and spat me right back out.

What the hell was I going to do? Not only could I lose my job, any scandal of this nature could—would—ruin Lucy's reputation on campus. Moreover, she had a great opportunity in front of her...one I hadn't even known about. Alison's threat was clear, if I made any hint at having any sort of relationship with Lucy that wasn't above board, she could kiss the recommendation letter goodbye. I couldn't let that happen. I'd done enough leg work on Lucy to know how much she wanted to be a vet, and the idea of getting in the way of that dream, especially given how competitive getting into vet school was...all Lucy'd ever wanted to do was work with animals. I had to think, and think fast.

I smirked, looking Alison up and down. "I think you've misread the situation, gorgeous," I lied, even as the words burned my throat. "I am genuinely tired, and I want to give you my undivided attention when we do go out. Lucy's my legal responsibility, and so I of course worry about her feelings, even if she does have a small crush on me." I shrugged. "It's normal for a girl her age. I'm sorry for giving you the wrong impression."

Alison's face softened and warmed. "Of course," she practically cooed, and I had to force myself not to rip her hand off me when she placed it on my chest for the second time that night. I'd never physically hurt a woman before and I wasn't going to start now, as much as I wanted to recoil from her touch. "It must be difficult to be a man in your position. You're doing a good thing, and yes, it is normal for a girl her age to develop inappropriate feelings for men in positions of authority. Another night then!"

She sashayed away from me, like she expected me to watch her ass, but I didn't. I was too busy trying to figure out a way to think myself out of this mess.

Next to me, Trey cleared his throat. I'd forgotten he was even there.

"You know," he said. "My sister's right."

"Trey, I'm tired," I sighed.

And I needed to find Lucy and make sure she listened to me. Even if I wasn't sure what to tell her.

"You've always done the right thing," he continued, ignoring me. "By the team, by Lucy. I know things have gotten...complicated," he snorted. "It's obvious. But you're skating on thin ice here, and you know it. How many lives are you going to destroy if you follow your dick instead of your head?"

It wasn't my dick I was following.

It was my heart.

But I didn't say that to him.

I deflected instead.

"You and your sister both misread the entire situation," I told him. "I'm exhausted. I'm going home. I'll see you tomorrow at film study. We won, but not by enough, and I need to make sure we're prepared for game two."

"Sure," he said. As I turned to leave, he had a parting shot. "If you really care about Lucy, doesn't what she needs matter more than what she wants?"

I kept walking.

♥.♥

THERE WAS A PROBLEM.

When I got to the parking lot, my keys were missing.

Shit.

I retraced my steps. Had I left them in my office? The locker room? Dropped them somewhere?

But the memory of Lucy reaching in my pocket earlier came back to me.

I grimaced.

She'd been kicked out of her second boarding school for

being a pickpocket. I should've realized, but at the moment I'd been too busy trying to keep control of my cock to notice her stealing my keys. Her barely there touch had been too arousing, at the worst possible time. It certainly didn't occur to me she had an ulterior motive.

She'd taken my car...but why? And gone where?

I pulled up the GPS app and pulled up her dot on the map. She was already headed out of Gehenom, going south down Route 13...I wasn't sure where to. The city?

I needed to follow her. I didn't care how expensive it was going to be, I ordered a rideshare off the app.

I was going to find Lucy and give her the apology and explanation she deserved. Hell, she deserved more than I could give her, but I'd give her everything I had, if it meant she'd listen to me. If it meant she'd give me a chance to make things right. And then I'd finally get my lips on hers, prove it to her with the kiss I owed her, and everything else I owed her. Because you kissed women you loved. And fuck me, I loved that little troublemaker. I wasn't giving her up, no matter what. Even if both our lives went to hell in the process.

I was drunk.

Not tipsy. Not toasted. Completely, utterly, floor-spinning-around, forget-my-own-name, happy-loud-funny-sad, drunk.

I was also at a bar in the middle of Nowheresville, New York, somewhere between the Finger Lakes and the city, without much cell service, or more than ten dollars and a very easily traceable credit card to my name.

I was an idiot, but I was having fun.

I mean, I was pretending to have fun.

Was I?

Right.

The guys on either side of me were clearly having fun. They'd started out buying me shots, then moved in closer, then closer still, playing it easy and lowkey at first as they asked me questions about myself.

Then the flirting started.

Then the touching.

I usually wasn't this fucking stupid, but I was too drunk

and pissed off to resist when one stroked the skin above my shorts and under my jersey, and the other rested a hand on my bare thigh.

I felt sick, disloyal, I didn't want their hands on me, the man whose hands I wanted probably had them on someone else by now. And if I thought about Coach and Alison on that date, I'd either scream or puke.

So instead of ripping their hands off me, I sat and laughed at their dumb jokes while the room spun and I tried not to vomit all over the peanut-shell-covered bar floor.

"You okay, honey?" the bartender asked me for probably the fourth time that night, eyeing my empty shot glasses and my unwelcome companions.

Oh god, no.

I *was* going to puke.

"Nope," I announced, practically falling off the barstool and not saying a word to either man as I passed them and headed down the hallway.

I barely made it to the bathroom before I was retching in the toilet, everything—all the alcohol, all my helpless anger, my loneliness and yearning—going straight into the toilet. I think I puked tears, too, if that was a thing. Because the alcohol had failed to fill in the hole in my chest where my heart had been, the heart that Coach had ripped out and stepped all over when he told Alison they were going to be late for their reservation.

When I was done vomiting—and believe me, it took a while before I got all of that sickness and sadness out—I felt marginally better.

Marginally.

I stood, shaky and lightheaded but at least planted on a

solid ground, and made my way over to the sink. I washed my hands, rinsed out my mouth, and splashed water all over my splotchy, rose-hued face.

"What the fuck are you doing, Lucy?" I asked my reflection. "How did you sink this low?"

My reflection didn't have an answer. She just looked confused. Disappointed. *Broken*. She didn't want to have this conversation with me, she wanted to be back in Coach's arms.

"Well tough luck, buttercup," I told my reflection. "He doesn't want us, and we know better than to go where we're not wanted, don't we?"

Time to blow this popsicle stand. I was in no shape to drive—I knew that much—so I'd have to sleep in Blake's car for the night. I grimaced. He was going to kill me when he realized I'd committed grand theft auto and stolen his prized Lexus. But then, he was probably too busy with whatsherface to realize it was gone...

I pushed my way out of the bathroom, only to be blocked by the two men who'd been feeding me drinks all night.

Oh, fuck.

"Excuse me," I said brightly, or as brightly as I could manage. "I appreciated the company, but I think it's time I head out."

"Ah, but the fun's just getting started," one drawled.

The other grabbed me by the wrist, gripping tight. "And you owe us for all the drinks...you aren't going anywhere, are you, Lacy?"

Seriously? This was the last thing my drunk ass needed right now.

"I am," I said. "Home."

"Oh, we'll take you home, alright" the first said as they pushed in closer to me.

I tried to shift around, to evade, but dread filled me. I opened my mouth to scream, only for one of them to cover it with his big, meaty hand.

It stunk. It was nothing like when Blake had covered my mouth with his hand to keep anyone from hearing me come.

Oh god, I wanted Blake.

I also wanted to puke again.

So I did, letting vomit soak the man's hand.

"What the actual fuck, oh you drunk bitch," he snapped as he wrenched his hand away. I used the distraction to get around them and run away, but the other hadn't released my wrist, and instead I felt something twist.

I screamed in pain and anger, turning to punch one of those assholes with my other hand, somehow...

But my wrist was suddenly free, and I was free.

There was an unholy, almost animalistic roar and then the sound of fists on flesh. Yelps and screams. I cradled my wrist, trying to see in the dark. Had they been mauled by an animal? There were bears up here...but who let a bear into a bar?

Always choose the bear, right? Maybe the bartender knew.

Fuck, I was still drunk and confused as hell by what was happening, even though I was relieved to be free of those assholes.

Pulling my phone out of my pocket with the hand that didn't hurt, I thumbed on the flashlight and shone it...only to gasp.

Because the bear in question was Blake, beating the shit out of the two men who'd tried to hurt me.

"Coach?" I asked in a whimper through the pain.

He paused for a second. He was splattered in blood, and the men on the ground weren't moving.

"Are you okay?" he asked, his voice guttural, almost inhuman.

"I—"

"They hurt you," he said flatly, and then he was back to beating both of them to a pulp.

"Coach, you need to stop. You'll kill them."

He shook his head. "Oh, I'll do much worse, sweetheart. Come here."

I stumbled over to him, trying not to gag at how much blood was everywhere.

The men were moaning, gasping for breath. On death's door.

I was grossed out by the blood, but I wasn't worried for them, not at all. Instead, all I felt was satisfaction.

They'd planned to hurt me, they had hurt me, and now they were paying for their crimes.

"What's wrong with your wrist?"

"I don't know, I think he broke it."

"Which one?"

I nodded to the one who was trying to crawl away.

And then shut my eyes when Coach stopped him with a shoe to the guy's crotch, pushing down until a scream split through the air.

"You can't kill them," I said, a little drunk and a lot reluctant. "You'll get sent to prison, and I'll be all alone."

Coach stopped, lifting his foot.

"You're lucky," he told the whimpering mess of a man on the ground. "That keeping her close matters more to me than sending you to hell. But I'll be watching, I guarantee it.

You try this with any other woman, I'll have no remorse over finishing the job."

Then, he was lifting me with his bloody hands and carrying me like a bride to the car.

"Thank you," I mumbled.

"You aren't going to thank me when I take this out on your bare ass," he muttered. "I'll give you a reprieve because you're going to have one hell of a hangover, but you have a lot of punishment coming your way."

"Yum," I mumbled, snuggling into his arms. "You smell good."

He snorted. "I doubt it."

"You smell like blood and rage and like you want to protect me," I slurred the words. "You know what's funny?"

He was still carrying me, and even though I could feel tension in his body, his arms were gentle.

"What's funny?"

"Earlier, I thought you might be a bear attacking them. Guess I picked the bear."

He pressed his lips to my hair.

"Guess you did."

And then I was out like a light.

♥‚♥

WHEN I OPENED MY EYES, IT WAS TO BRIGHT, GLARING LIGHTS that hurt my head, loud beeps, and serious-sounding murmurs. Even though I wasn't on my own two feet, I was moving, and I still wanted to puke.

I glanced up at the wall of chest holding me. I could smell peat and honey, and the familiar scent immediately put me at ease. Blake. It was Blake holding me, Blake carrying me.

"Blake, what's going on? Where are we?"

He chuffed. "I brought you to the nearest hospital so they could take a look at your wrist...and make sure you don't die from alcohol poisoning. Seriously, Lucy, how much did you have to drink?"

I tried to count, and failed.

"A lot?" I guessed.

He snorted. "Well, that's helpful."

I relaxed into his arms. I was tall, curvy, and had never been carried around by a man before. It felt good, being held this way, like I was delicate and needed attention and care.

What had Blake called me that day?

"The most important thing," he hummed, like he'd heard my thoughts. "And I've done a bad job looking after you so far. I'll do better."

It sounded like a promise, the kind that made my chest warm and my feet tingle. It was a *good* promise, even though he hadn't followed through on many of his promises so far. That thought sobered me up enough that when we reached the triage nurse's desk, I didn't seem as drunk as I actually was...hopefully.

The nurse looked up at us, and up, and up. She took my sorry appearance in, and I'm sure all the magnificence that was Blake, and sat up in her chair.

"What are you here for?"

"Some asshole twisted her wrist. Maybe broke it. And she's been drinking and I want a toxicology report to make sure she doesn't need her stomach pumped or to be observed overnight."

Her brows shot up, and she looked immediately suspicious. "And are you the asshole who twisted her wrist?"

"No!" I said, shaking my head and hitting Blake's chest with my hair. I stared down at the nurse. "I got into trouble with some gross dudes at a bar and they hurt me when I tried to escape. Blake rescued me."

She didn't look convinced, but she nodded at a clipboard with papers on it. "Fill that out, and make sure you give back the pen. Hospital's short on funds, and even the pen budget could get slashed next year."

With that, she dismissed us. Blake carried me over to a set of plastic chairs in the waiting area, carefully setting me down in one before sitting in the other.

I looked at my left wrist, completely out of commission.

"If I give you my information, can you write it down for me?" I asked pitifully. "I don't know my insurance information off the top of my head—"

"I know it," he interrupted as he started filling out the form.

"—but it should be in my purse...wait, you know it?"

Blake glanced at me, and his hard face softened. "Sweetheart, I have it memorized. I always worried you might end up in an emergency situation, and I wanted to be prepared. I know your full name, date of birth, address, insurance information...the only thing I don't know is your social security number and the date of your last period." He laughed. "And sometimes I feel like I'm crazy, because I want to know those things, too. Like if I know everything there is to know about you, I'll be able to keep you safe. Unlike tonight. I'm so sorry, Lucy."

That same warmth encompassed my chest, my toes kept tingling. He may not be holding me, but I could feel him around me. This was attention. This was care. Maybe he got too stuck in trying to be the right guy for me, but it was clear —I mattered to him. In a way I often worried I'd never mattered to anyone.

"You did keep me safe. If you hadn't shown up..."

"I don't even want to think about what would have happened if I hadn't been there. But I didn't get there in time, and if I had been quicker on my feet, this wouldn't have happened in the first place," he said. "I didn't keep you safe—if I did, you wouldn't be holding your wrist like that right now."

He was right. I was cradling my wrist to ease some of the pain. But he was wrong about not keeping me safe. Because I'd never felt safer.

He finished the forms.

"Don't go anywhere, Lucy," he said, waiting until I nodded in agreement.

"Yes, daddy," I said quietly, and his eyes lit up.

He bent down and kissed my hair, then bent lower and pressed his lips to my cheek, sending those toe tingles up through the rest of my body. Before he stood, he whispered in my ear, "I need to kiss you for real, but if I do we're going to make a scene in the ER."

With those words, he walked away, leaving me feeling like I needed a defibrillator. Who knew it took stealing his car and getting stupid drunk to get him to tell me he wanted to kiss me?

I watched him as he walked back to the desk to give the forms to the nurse. He walked like he meant business, but then he always walked like he meant business. His long legs ate up the floor, his narrow hips and perfect bubble butt impossible to look away from. His back was straight but relaxed, his broad shoulders taking up the entire room. Everything about him screamed power, confidence, and charisma. He was a magnet everyone was drawn to, and I couldn't help but feel special that he was drawn to me.

I need to kiss you for real, but if I do, we'll make a scene in the ER.

Whatever conversation with the nurse was taking awhile, but then Blake settled back into the chair next to mine, his leg pressing against mine. It had done that earlier tonight at the game too, but this time it wasn't accompanied with the fear of him going on a date with someone else.

What had happened with that?

"Was Professor Putrovski upset that you bailed on your date early to find me?"

He glanced at me. "There was no date."

Psh. "Could've fooled me," I said, not wanting him to see how relieved I was.

"Lucy, I only went along with it to protect you. You have to know that, don't you? That woman has so much power over your future, and I refuse to risk you losing out on any opportunity that gets you closer to your goals. I had to distract her, but you were gone before I could explain."

Oh.

Well, duh.

Part of me had assumed as much, but the deep hurt from my past had been too loud. And it was hard to completely blame myself when he'd been so hot and cold with me. How was I supposed to know he was trying to protect me and not that he wanted to go out with a beautiful, age-appropriate woman?

"Troublemaker," he said quietly and calmly, "Come here."

"Where?" I asked, confused.

He patted his lap.

"Where I know you aren't going anywhere, and I can feel

with my own body you're alright," he said, not that he needed to.

I was already climbing off the seat and moving over to sit on him. I'd barely bent my knees when I was being pulled gently backward and down, until I was on his lap, my ass resting above his cock, my bare legs layered over his slacks, my feet on top of his. He pulled me deeper into his chest, resting his head on top of mine. I both felt and heard his sigh as he wrapped his arms around my waist and seemed to finally relax.

"There we go, that's better," he said. "Daddy's got you now."

I wriggled at his words, even with the ache in my wrist, and his cock hardened underneath me right between my ass cheeks. The brush of it sent pleasant, unfamiliar shocks through my belly. I'd never realized that pressure there could feel good, but—

"Yeah, we're going to have to save that for later, sweetheart," he growled.

"We need to talk about all of this," I reminded him.

"You mean, you stealing my car and running away like a brat?" he said.

"Or you bugging my room and stealing my underwear like a creep," I shot back, being careful to keep my voice down.

"Yeah, that too."

But before we could get into it, my name was called.

I glanced around the ER waiting room. There was a man with blood all over his face and neck, a woman holding a red, screaming baby.

"How are we already up? There's no way she thought my wrist was more serious than what's going on with all these other people, and they've been here a lot longer than we have," I protested.

"I may have bribed her," he said, nudging me to stand.

I rose. "Coach Samson, you *bribed* someone? Who are you?"

He took my hand. "Someone who realized how close he came to losing what mattered most," he said, leaving me speechless for the first time in my life as he tugged me out of the room and down the hallway to where a medical technician waited to lead us into a room.

We didn't wait long when another nurse appeared to take my vitals. Blake was quiet, a serious, protective, looming presence as she checked my heart rate, temperature, and blood pressure before taking some notes and leaving us alone. Blake remained quiet when the doctor showed up minutes later.

"Lucy?" the doctor was an attractive man, or I would've thought so if Blake wasn't in the room.

"That's me," I said, brightly and a little drunkenly. Blake looked the doctor over, and his lips flattened and he moved further inside.

"I see," the doctor said kindly. He glanced at Blake wearily. "And you must be her father."

Damn it. I expected Blake to turn red or retreat emotionally from the reminder of our age difference and legal relationship, but he seemed to shrug it right off, standing at his full height like a reminder to the doctor of who the bigger man was.

"I'm her partner," he corrected, and I fought not to gasp. Or faint.

Partner?

"Since when?" I asked, unable to help myself.

"Since the hotel," Blake said gruffly.

"Well, Lucy's partner, I'll need to examine Lucy without you in the room."

No, what he needed to do was ask me if Blake had been the one to fuck up my wrist without him in the room, but I didn't feel the need to point out the obvious.

"I'm not leaving," Blake said resolutely.

I looked at him. "Blake, it's okay. Let me talk to the doctor real quick, and you can come right back in."

It was like trying to pacify a bull. Blake shook his head, but I raised my chin, staring him down. Finally, he relented.

"Two minutes," he told the doctor. "Don't make her uncomfortable."

The doctor looked affronted. "I'm not planning on it," he said, and with one last look at me, Blake left the room.

The moment he was gone, the doctor relaxed.

"He's a little old for you, isn't he?" he said.

I felt like a cat with my hackles up. I didn't need to hear that, and neither did Blake. Not when we were finally, *finally* getting somewhere.

"Please don't say that when he comes back in," I told the doctor earnestly. "He already feels bad enough about the power dynamic. I don't need him questioning our relationship."

The doctor laughed, surprised. "Alright. Well, I have to ask you some questions anyway."

"No, he didn't hurt me. I was pissed at him about...something, so I went to a bar, got too drunk, and these two creepy weirdos attacked me. Blake found me and rescued me before things could go too far. They're who fucked up my wrist."

The doctor's eyes widened. "Do you need to file a police report? I can get them to—"

"No." Who knew what they would do to Blake for going

to town on those men's faces. There was protection and there was full on vengeful rage, and I had a feeling the police wouldn't take kindly to the latter.

"Alright." He cleared his throat. "Lucy, do you feel safe in your relationship?"

That was easy. "Safer than I've ever felt in my entire life."

The doctor nodded.

"Now, can you let him back in? I want him with me," I told the doctor, and he went to open the door.

Blake stormed back into the room, stopping as soon as he saw me.

"I'm fine," I told him immediately to calm him, still unable to come to terms with the fact that Blake could lose his cool, much less that I could calm him down.

"I don't like leaving you alone," he explained, and then waited as the doctor gently checked over my wrist. He declared it sprained, fitted me for a brace, and wrote me a prescription for pain medication, telling me I couldn't take them until I sobered up tomorrow.

"What about potential alcohol poisoning?" Blake asked, clearly still worried.

The doctor laughed. "She seems completely coherent to me. Drink water, Lucy, you're going to have a hell of a hangover tomorrow, but I think you'll otherwise be alright. You're clearly in good hands."

With that, he left the room, and me alone with Blake.

"Can I go home?" I asked him, suddenly exhausted.

His eyes went dark.

"We're not going all the way back to Gehenom tonight. I rented us a last-minute Airbnb, we'll stay there for the night."

That sounded good to me. I let Blake lead me out of the hospital and back to his car.

"How did you even get to me?" I asked him.

"Mason gave me a ride."

Whoops.

"It's okay," Blake said to my unanswered question. "Let's just get you to the cabin and in bed, we'll deal with the rest in the morning."

Dealing with the rest in the morning sounded good to me.

Especially because I fell asleep to Blake buckling my seat belt in his car.

·

O *h god.*

Everything fucking hurt.

My head, my body…my left wrist.

I opened my eyes to the room swimming in front of me. I blinked, and everything straightened out.

Coach sat in a chair facing me in an unfamiliar bedroom.

Where was I?

I glanced down at the brace around my wrist.

Oh, right.

The night before came flooding back: Wearing Emory's jersey to the hockey game, Blake benching him temporarily, finding out about his "date" with my professor, stealing his car and ending up at a random bar halfway between Gehenom and New York City, getting attacked by those men, his rescue, the hospital. A lot had happened in very little time, and all were things I needed to parse through, both on my own and in a deep and probably heavy conversation with Blake himself.

Speaking of which…

"Every time I look at that brace, I want to kill those men all over again," he growled. Even with as nauseous as I felt, the growling was still hot.

I tried to sit up too quickly, and the room spun around me.

Blake was suddenly out of his chair, gently but with firm hands on my shoulders, lowering me back down to the bed.

"I thought you didn't kill them," I said.

He stared at me, face impassive. "Not for you to worry about."

"Okay, but I am worried about it. What did you do, Blake?"

"I went back to the bar, hunted them down, and finished the job." He shrugged like it was nothing. "Called in a favor. Like I said, it's nothing for you to worry about."

"You...you jeopardized your entire career? Your freedom? For me?"

"Troublemaker, sweetheart...don't you get it?" His face softened and he brushed hair out of my face. "I'd do absolutely anything for you. Cross any line. Killing some assholes who hurt you doesn't even come close to it."

"Oh."

I wanted to soak up his words, maybe record them so I could listen to them over and over, but right now I felt too nauseous to do anything but close my eyes.

"You need to sleep some more," he said from somewhere above me. "You're hungover."

"Where are we?"

He handed me painkillers and an open bottle of water.

"Airbnb I rented. I wanted us to have some time together away from campus so you could heal."

"But the team—"

"Trey's taking care of them. You're more important."

You're more important.

They were the three prettiest words in the English language, even if they weren't the ones I longed to hear from him. I'd never been more important than anything or anyone before. Not to my parents, not to my friends, and as far as I knew, not to Blake.

"I'll let you rest."

I immediately opened my eyes and put my hand on his. "Don't leave me."

He snorted. "Wasn't planning on it. Aside from taking care of those assholes, I'm not letting you out of my sight. Might even get you a leash and collar."

Even though I felt awful, my pussy clenched at the words.

His eyes darkened, but all he said was, "Trouble."

"Can you..."

I didn't have to finish the thought. He nodded, and then he was lifting the comforter, sliding into the bed, and gently pulling me into his arms.

I settled against him, sighing.

"How long do I get a reprieve for?"

"Until I'm sure you feel well enough to take what's coming your way," he said, the threat dark and delicious.

Sighing, I shut my eyes and fell right back asleep.

♥⸳♥

THE NEXT TIME I WOKE UP, I WAS FACE DOWN, ASS UP ON Blake's lap—and trussed up like a chicken. My arms were tied to my sides, my bare breasts pressed against his thigh. My legs were fully bent on either side, shins and ankles tied tight to my thighs, and then another rope went around my shins, forcing me into a frog-like position. I was open, available, and vulnerable, my pussy and ass exposed for anything and everything that Coach wanted. My stomach and core spun tight and sweet at the thought, like I was woven in cotton candy and not rope.

Was this a very sexy dream?

"What the fuck?" I asked, groggily...

...until a smack sounded and my right ass cheek burned.

There went the grogginess.

"What the hell, Blake? What happened to kissing the princess awake instead of spanking her?"

"The princess—"

Smack.

"Didn't steal the knight's car—"

Smack.

"Ignore her phone—"

Smack.

"And get drunk out in the middle of nowhere where anything could—and almost did—happen to her."

Smack. Smack. Smack.

My asscheeks stung, my whole body was hot...

...and I was already soaking his thigh.

I pretended it wasn't happening. "Are you victim blaming me?"

His hand stopped peppering my ass with spanks, and he sighed.

"You're right, that was shitty. What those men almost did was gross and not your fault. But you still put yourself at risk, and I'm unwilling to let that go. The reckless decision-making has to end, Lucy. I know you did it because you wanted my attention, but you've got it now."

I glared at the floor.

"You think I ran off because I wanted your attention? No,

I left because I was angry because you had fucked me but were about to go on a date with another woman. Can you untie me while we have this conversation?"

Blake lifted me up so I could face him, placing me on his lap.

"I was never going to go on a date with another woman," he said, voice solid. "We've discussed this already."

"I know that now, but then..." I could remember the way she'd touched his chest, and it still burned in my own. So I took a big risk, my voice trembling, unable to look him in the eyes as I whispered, "It *hurt*, Blake."

Blake gripped my chin, turning it back to him.

"Sweetheart, I promise you, I never was going to go on a date with her. There are no other women. I haven't been able to get hard for anyone else since you came sashaying back into my life during orientation."

"You hurt me," I repeated.

He sighed, kissing my forehead. "I know."

"And I was pissed."

He kissed my forehead again. "I know that, too. But that's no excuse to put yourself at risk. I'd rather you have bitched me out in public, slapped me, thrown something at me, than gone running off like you did."

"Noted. So can you untie me?"

He shook his head.

"No. Because I need to punish us both. And a spanking isn't going to do anything but excite us. This is a teachable moment."

He rose, depositing me back on the bed, still trussed up and unable to go anywhere or do anything but watch as he shook out his hands and showed them to me. His knuckles were cracked, a little bruised...probably from beating the shit out of and possibly killing those men last night. I tried to feel bad about it, but I still felt nothing but satisfaction. What that said about me, I wasn't entirely sure, but then I was a woman who had little to no recourse in this society when it came to men who wanted to hurt me, so having someone in my corner who was willing to get the revenge I so sorely needed felt too good to deny. If that made me bad, well...it was nothing new.

I hated that he'd bruised up his hand though.

"Does it hurt?" I asked.

He gave me a wry smile.

"Not yet."

Then he approached the wall next to the mirror.

"God, this is going to cost me a fuck ton of money—and destroy my rating on this damn site," he muttered.

Worry pooled in my stomach.

"Coach. Blake. What are you about to do?"

"Do you have any idea what it was like, Lucy, knowing you were somewhere, possibly unsafe, and that I might not get to you in time? And then finding you in that dark hall at the bar with those men's hands on you? Knowing it was my fault that you were in that position in the first place?"

"No..." I trailed off. "Blake."

He made a fist out of his left hand, thumb on the outside, and glanced behind him to look at me.

"It was the worst feeling in the world. The terror literally *hurt*...more than this is going to."

And then he motherfucking punched a hole in the wall.

I screamed.

And then I screamed again.

"No, stop it!"

The sounds—my scream and the impact of bone and flesh on sheetrock and plaster—echoed in the room, making my chest squeeze tight. I couldn't breathe.

"What the fuck, Blake?! Stop!"

"No."

He punched the wall again.

And again.

"I'll stop when you get it. When you understand what you're being punished for, and you understand how it feels when someone you—someone you care about is hurt."

I tried to wiggle off the bed and go to him, to stop him, to make this horror stop, but I couldn't. My arms burned as I tried to pull them free, my legs, too. I could do *nothing*. Absolutely *nothing*. I cried then, completely helpless, forced to watch him hurt himself, and that helplessness was too much to bear, so I shut my eyes instead.

"Lucy, if you don't fucking open your eyes and watch me right now, I'll drag you to the kitchen and you can watch while I set my hand on fucking fire."

My eyes shot open.

He watched me in the mirror as he punched, and punched, and punched, not making a single sound of pain, blood seeping between his knuckles and painting the white wall.

"Please, please, stop," I begged, full on sobbing now. "Stop it, stop it."

"No, I deserve this as much as you do. I deserve it for not being honest with you and hurting you, and you deserve it for not being honest with me and hurting yourself."

"Blake, stop, I'll do anything, I swear to god, just stop, I'm so sorry, I'm so sorry, I promise I won't be reckless anymore, I won't do bad shit to get your attention, just please stop..."

He stopped immediately, shaking out his bloody hand.

"Motherfucker, that hurt," he muttered, and then he was crossing the room toward me and lifting me with up with both hands, one clean, one bloody, getting his blood on me. And I hated it, hated him, and hated myself more.

"I hate you," I told him.

His eyes were gentle.

"No you don't."

"I do."

"You don't, Lucy. If you did, you wouldn't care. This wouldn't have hurt you. I won't make you say the words now, but we both know how you really feel."

He sat down, placing me on his lap so I straddled him, and rocked me, and I let him, even though he was getting blood everywhere, because I couldn't stop him, and because after everything he'd just done, being held this way felt soothing in ways I'd never known I needed.

Finally, I said, "Can you untie me now?"

He stroked a bloody hand over my back, leaving remnants of his guilt and atonement all over my body.

"Not until I do this first," he said, and as he leaned toward me and tilted his head down, my breath caught.

Was he about to...?

"Blake..."

"God," he groaned, his lips practically touching mine so we were breathing the same air. "I've been dreaming about this for so long. You know I've never done this before, right?"

My heart stopped.

"Wait, what are—"

But before I could finish my question, he kissed me.

And I lost my breath entirely.

He was gentle at first, a barely there brush of his lips against mine, once, twice, three times, before he rested his mouth on top of mine, breathing slowly. Just touching, nothing more, but the softness and the slowness cracked open something inside me, and a seed planted so, so long ago, but had never seen light, began to bloom.

As it unfurled, so did my heart, with the sweetest ache. Tears came to my eyes, and he must have felt them as they dripped down between our faces, because he pulled back and brushed my hair out of the way, looking at me.

"Sweetheart, what's wrong?" he asked.

"Not what's wrong, what's right," I said, leaning back in and trying to capture his lips with mine again, frustrated that I couldn't move my arms to grab him around his neck and pull him toward me. I had no choice but to take what he gave me. And what he gave me was slow and steady, tender and caring, solid and sweet. I inhaled the peat and honey scent of him as he kissed me again, harder this time.

"Open your mouth, Lucy," he said against my lips, and I did. Immediately, he surged inside, his tongue thrusting and licking into my mouth, groaning as he clutched me tighter. He tasted so good, fresh mint and honey, and I chased his taste, chased his tongue, completely uninterested in being demure or coy, fully invested in tasting as much of him as I could. He tasted me right back, his tongue tracing patterns on the inside of my mouth before going to war with my tongue, doing his best to dominate mine. I fought back, but he fought harder and won, forcing me into submission as he took, and gave, and I gave, and took, forgetting everything and everyone until all that existed in this moment was his mouth and mine. A supernova began to form inside me, my thighs wet with need and my body burning bright as he declared me his with every lick, every kiss, every bite of my lips.

"Mine," he growled against my mouth.

"Mine," I growled right back.

He laughed, the feeling resonating through my whole

body, and, without warning, bright light exploded behind my eyes as I came from nothing but a kiss, writhing in his lap, riding him, his pants the only barrier between my opening and his cock.

Finally, he pulled away, breathing heavily.

"Oh, sweetheart, that was better than anything I could have imagined," he said.

"Was that really your first kiss?"

He nodded. "You were my first—and you'll be my last."

Oh.

My.

God.

"Can you untie me now?" I asked again, gasping.

This time, when he laughed, it was dark, not sweet, and filled with depraved promises I knew he'd fulfill.

He stroked a bloody hand over my back.

"Not until after I fuck you," he said. "And sweetheart, after that kiss, it's going to be hard and long and relentless, so I hope you're ready."

I wasn't.

28

BLAKE

Although the kiss had been so overwhelming, so incredible, so out-of-this-goddamn-world it blocked out everything else, now that I'd put Lucy back on the bed and was in the bathroom patching myself up, the pain came back. My hand hurt like a bitch.

But then, I'd been a real bitch.

I'd made a decision the night before, to protect myself and Lucy from scandal—and it had backfired spectacularly. When I found her in that dark hallway at that bar, helpless and hurt, anger like I'd never felt took over until any semblance of control was gone and all I saw was red. I'd beat those men so violently and forcefully, I'd almost killed them. And then I had gone back and actually killed them. I'd probably be in a cell right now if I hadn't called Micah Feldman, who said he and his brother Marcus would "take care of it," whatever that meant. I didn't worry about it, all my attention on getting back to Lucy. And I'd introduced myself as her partner because from now on, that's what I was.

From the moment she'd walked away from me after the

hockey game to rescuing her, all the doubts and fears had... well, they hadn't entirely gone away, but they stopped mattering. She mattered. I loved her. And I wasn't letting her go.

I thought I'd delivered the punishment to both of us well enough, the lesson had been learned, her kiss had set me on fire, and all I wanted—other than some goddamn Advil for my hand—was to get my cock so deep inside of Lucy's pussy, we both forgot that we'd ever been two separate people.

As I cleaned my hand and applied salve to it in the bathroom, I glanced over at her. She lay on her back on the bed, legs frog tied open so her rose-pink pussy was visible, arms at her sides, rope wound round and around to protect her wrist from further damage. The position pushed her heaving chest forward, nipples pointing up at the ceiling.

She might still be pissed at me—and herself—but she was turned on by all of this. And she'd come in my lap from kissing me alone, the single hottest thing that had ever happened in my whole goddamn life, including the other times I'd fucked her.

Fuck, that kiss.

I'd be replaying it in my head for the rest of my life. And I bet, even when I was old and gray and Lucy was pushing me around in a wheelchair, I'd still get hard thinking about it.

Once my hand was taken care of—the second time I'd had to clean and bandage my hand because of Lucy—I rummaged through the shopping bag. I'd gone on a little expedition this morning to a sex shop and grabbed some necessary provisions.

Pulling out lube, nipple clamps, a clit sucking vibrator in the shape of a flower, and a vibrating butt plug, I paused at the dildo-shaped gag. Lucy had been a virgin only a couple weeks ago, and I was springing all sorts of shit on her. Was I throwing her into the deep end too quickly? What's more, with her tied up and gagged, she'd have no way to use her safe word.

Who the fuck was I?

The guilt spiral started right on time when she sweetly called, "Blake, are you going to leave me here like this forever, you asshole?"

Well, slightly sweetly.

But it pulled me out of my spiral.

Lucy was an adult. She needed me, needed someone to call the shots and make it clear how much she was wanted. I'd make it good for her. And we'd figure out the rest later.

I entered the bedroom and dropped everything I'd bought on her stomach.

"Lucy," I said, trying to sound easy about what I needed to know, "I'm about to ask you a question, and I need you to answer me completely honestly. I will not be upset, whatever you say, and I need you to understand that, okay?"

She looked up at me, lifting her head to glance at what I'd bought.

"Oh, shit," she gasped. "Did you hack my Kindle or something?"

I processed that sentence.

"What do you mean?"

A blush rose across her body, completely captivating me. Fuck me, she was pink *everywhere*.

"This is the...I fantasize about this stuff a lot when I get off," she said, and I could tell that even though she was trying to be nonchalant, saying it out loud embarrassed her.

"Is that so?" I stroked a small, light circle around her belly button, pleased when she writhed underneath me. Even more pleased that we were on the same page, sexually.

It was like she'd been made for me, like I'd dreamed her up one day, and the universe decided to make her real. I wasn't sure what I'd done to deserve her, but I was keeping her, regardless. No take backs.

"Yeah, although I wasn't hogtied in those fantasies…"

"Do you not want to be?"

She swallowed, staring me in the eye. "I want everything with you."

My heart thumped, hard.

I want everything with you, too, I thought, but didn't—couldn't—tell her.

Not yet.

Not until I'd figured out how to keep her and still give her everything she wanted.

"Lucy, I want you completely under my control. I want to tie you up and gag you and force you to come until it hurts, and then fuck you until it hurts some more. But that means you won't be able to say your safe word. That means you're going to have to completely trust me, and I'm going to have to trust myself to not fuck up."

"Fuck," she whimpered, and I watched, riveted, as her hips pumped the air at my words alone, wetness appearing and coating her thighs.

"Is that 'fuck' a 'yes?'"

"Yes. Take away my control, Coach—I never had it around you to begin with, anyway."

My cock went hard at her words.

"Keep your eyes on me, sweetheart. I want to see them the whole time."

She nodded, and I leaned over her.

"Open your mouth. Like you would for my cock."

She opened her mouth, licking her lips, and I slowly slid the dildo gag in. It wasn't as long or thick as me, so it wouldn't choke her, but it would keep her mouth busy and full while I went to work on the rest of her.

Carefully, I buckled the rubber straps around her head, gently pulling her hair loose so it rested in a beautiful golden mess on the pillow. The night I'd brought her home, her hair had been that same shining chaos, bringing light to my dark life, and god, I wanted it back. I wanted it—her—there, forever.

Lost in that image, I absently stroked her cheek, picturing what it would be like to have Lucy in my life. Her pink everything everywhere, messy closet, noise and laughter, that sunshine-and-sex smell permeating every inch of my house. I'd never wanted anything like I wanted that, and I was determined to have it.

How, I wasn't sure yet. So I chose to ignore that worry, focusing on my fingers brushing over her silky soft cheek, watching as she shivered, pressing a kiss to her forehead and then concentrating on what came next.

Lifting the nipple clamps, I rained kisses down her face and to her neck, focusing on the tender spot between her neck and shoulder—the one that made her chest rise fast and the pink on her chest turn a brighter, deeper hue, then turned my attention to her nipples. I drew small circles on one, then the other, first with my thumb, then with my tongue, taking my time until they were pointy and so sensitive her whole body jerked when I gently bit down.

"This is going to hurt a hell of a lot worse, little troublemaker," I warned as I brought the little nipple clamps to her chest, fixing one on, then the other. They had little bells that rang as she moved and shrieked at the shock of pain.

"Shhh," I crooned to her. "Shh. I know it hurts but you can handle it. I know you can. The pain will settle."

She sighed, and so did I, stroking her areolas, listening to her tits as they jingled as delightfully as her laugh.

Kissing my way down her body, I focused on her inner thighs, biting both, but ignoring her wet pussy. I was pretty damn heroic for being able to manage that, especially because I could smell her, sunshine and sex and pussy. She was everything I'd ever wanted and never dreamed I could have.

And then I opened the bottle of lube.

Lucy's eyes got big and she tried to say something, muffled by the rubber dick in her mouth.

I paused, scanning her to make sure she wasn't saying no.

"Okay?" I asked tenderly. "I'm not going to fuck that gorgeous ass—yet—but I want to fill you up there, too. It will feel good, I promise."

It would feel good for me too, with a vibrating plug in her ass and my cock in her pussy. My dick jerked in my pants in anticipation.

A small nod.

Good.

Flicking open the top of the bottle, I squeezed a liberal amount onto my fingers, slowly rimming her asshole with them. She writhed.

"Oh, sweetheart, shhh...I'm just getting started," I promised, before pushing one finger inside her tight, tiny little hole, just up to the knuckle.

She jerked, and I shushed her, soothing her as I slowly worked one finger in and out, marveling at the way she clamped on me, the heat there.

"Almost makes me want to fuck your ass today instead," I growled to myself, setting off a litany of muffled mewls.

"No, no, don't worry, little troublemaker. I have at least that much control."

For now.

But I kept that to myself.

Instead, I withdrew my finger, applying more lube, and then pushed two fingers in slowly but inexorably until they were deep inside, then scissoring them. With my free hand, I traced small circles on her inner thighs. Lucy trembled, clenching, and moaned around the gag.

"That's right, sweetheart. You're being such a good girl for daddy, aren't you?"

She nodded, eyes on mine, heating my whole body with her trust and submission.

Pulling them free, I lubed up the vibrating plug, then pushed it in, watching the way her gorgeous ass swallowed it up, all the way to the base.

I tapped the end of it, and she jumped.

Just to be a dick, I tapped the end of it again.

She jumped again.

"That feel good, sweetheart? You're about to feel much, much, better."

Bending down, I captured her little clit in my mouth, licking circles around it to coax it out from behind its hood. Lucy's little clit was a good girl—better behaved than the person she belonged to—because it only took a few circles with my tongue until she was out in the open...and vulnerable.

"Perfect," I said, meaning so much more than her hard clit, as I picked up the little flower toy.

"Do you know what this is?" I asked conversationally.

She nodded, looking like her heart was in her throat.

God, I wanted my cock to be in her throat. But there would be time for that later.

On that thought, I picked up the last thing—a vial of Vice, popped it open, and poured it down my own throat.

"Oh that's right, little troublemaker," I told her shocked gaze. "I have plans for your pussy, and they require a shorter refractory period than usual."

Remembering the little flower toy, I attached it to her protruding clit...and grabbed my phone, opening the app and setting both the butt plug and the flower toy to vibrate. And then, unzipping my pants, I pulled out my cock and sat down next to Lucy to watch the show.

29

LUCY

I'd never been more turned on in my life.

I'd never felt more vulnerable in my life.

And as scary as it was, I loved it.

The vibrations were almost too much to bear, but they were nothing compared to Blake's hand resting on my restrained thigh and his eyes on mine as I tried, and failed, to writhe. It was ecstasy and hell at the same time.

And I couldn't say a word.

God, I couldn't say a word. Couldn't beg for more, or for less, couldn't tell him no, couldn't tell him yes. I'd never put my trust and faith in someone so completely, but when he'd asked me, I hadn't questioned it for a second.

I didn't trust anyone.

But I trusted him.

I shouldn't, not after everything he'd done. But I knew on some level that Blake would never hurt me. Would shove a knife in his own chest before he risked my safety.

I'd do absolutely anything for you. Cross any line. Killing some assholes who hurt you doesn't even come close to it.

Yeah. So. I was tied up and unable to do anything but

submit to pleasure and moan into the gag, wishing it was his cock in my mouth, in my pussy, even in my ass, as scary as that sounded.

I was stretched wide, filled to the brim, my nipples sore and aching from the sharp bite of the clamps—and I loved it. Even though I hated it. Hated the way the vibrators forced one orgasm out of me, then another, without any rhythm or regularity as Blake turned the vibrators on higher and lower, slower and faster, based on some silent whims he didn't share with me. My body writhed and I trembled from both needing to come and needing to never come again, but not once did I take my eyes off his.

The expression in them was sublime. The green in them was like a forest at midnight, filled with frightening things I desperately wanted to explore, no matter how much it might hurt. They held lust in their depths, sure, a claim of ownership, of course, but also a softness that looked so close to love, I came again when I saw it.

By now, my pussy was clenching weakly, needy and empty. My ass was clenching too, but at least it had some-thing to grasp. Distantly, my breasts chimed from the bells on the clamps. I started begging, even though it came out as garbled nonsense.

"Oh, sweetheart, do you need something?" Coach asked, green eyes glinting. "Do you need to come again?"

He played with his phone, jacking the vibrations up so high I started screaming from the pleasure-pain. And still he didn't relent.

I started shaking my head, back and forth, pleading with my eyes for him to get rid of the vibrators and actually fuck me.

"You can take a few more," he murmured, kissing my sweaty cheek. "Just a few more for daddy, and then I'll give you my cock. There you go, that's one, that's a good girl. Let's get you another. Keep those gorgeous eyes on me while I torture you some more…"

He kept talking, but I couldn't hear him, my body too overwrought, overwhelmed, to do much more than float in the space between joy and suffering. He'd said only a few more, but I swear I must have orgasmed a thousand and one more times, seconds stretching into years as he crooned words to me I could barely hear.

Finally, finally, the buzzing stopped. I lay there in a weak daze as he removed the flower vibrator from my clit and released the clamps from my nipples, sending a shocking burn and then relief through me. He didn't remove the butt plug, but his hands lifted my head, working open the buckle and pulling the dildo gag free. I inhaled deeply, mouth dry from my moans and cries.

My hearing came back to me, and so did clarity.

"Poor little troublemaker." He tsked as he reached over to the nightstand and grabbed a bottle of water, holding my neck and head up with one hand while he popped off the lid and held it to my mouth with the other.

I drank greedily, the cool water bathing my insides and bringing me back to life. My whole body ached from the ropes and the orgasms.

"You're evil," I gasped. "That was evil."

He threw his head back and laughed, the sound so beautiful my heart ached with it. Blake so rarely laughed that each one was precious, and I swore I'd make him laugh every day for the rest of our lives.

"I'm not done being evil," he told me, and then he was standing and stripping off his shirt and pants, revealing a broad, muscular chest, lightly covered in hair, a six pack, narrow hips, and his huge, hard cock. Thick, tree-trunk thighs and muscular calves completed the masterpiece of his body. Even his feet were works of art.

Climbing onto the bed, he pressed one forearm next to my head, grabbing my left hip with the other and tugging me up, lining his cock up with my swollen opening, and then surging inside. I was so wet from the multiple orgasms he'd forced on me that he slid right in. Deep. Confident. Dominant. Sure. All the way until he bottomed out, resting his balls against my ass.

"Ah, fuck," he groaned as he stared into my eyes. "How is this pussy so goddamn perfect? How are you so goddamn perfect?"

Before I could come up with a sassy reply—my brain was a little slow from all the orgasms—he kissed me, seductive and brutal, conquering my mouth with his. I let him, I had no other choice. My eyes started to flutter closed, but then the vibrations started back up in my ass, and they popped wide open.

"Coach…"

"No, what do you call me?" he warned.

"Daddy…" I whined, but he ignored me, pulling out and shoving back in, hard and deep, snapping his hips with a breakneck pace I could've barely kept up with if I'd been able to move. As it was, tied up and energy depleted, I had no choice but to take his rough thrusts, lost in the juxtaposition of him mercilessly fucking my pussy as he stared tenderly into my eyes. I thought I'd felt full before, but between the plug in my ass and his cock in my cunt, it was like there was no room left inside me—Blake had taken over it all.

"Can you come for me again?"

"No," I begged.

"Just one more time, sweetheart. You can, I know you

can. You're so strong. You can do anything. Come for me, you gorgeous girl."

The praise did it. My whole body shook with the power of it, crying out into Blake's mouth as he swooped in for another kiss, swallowing the sound as he powered into me. He moaned into the kiss, his hips stuttering as wet heat filled me up inside, and then he stilled, slumping over my body, his heart pounding against mine.

"Fuck," he said.

That was the right thing to say.

A moment later, he slipped out of me, his cum following his exit. He rolled off of me, and then he was lifting me up and gently undoing the ropes, freeing each limb, one after another. My whole body tingled as blood rushed back to my limbs and Blake rubbed them to help with any soreness. Finally, he pulled the vibrator out of my ass. I immediately felt empty. I immediately wanted it back.

"Fuck," he said again, staring at it.

"What?" I asked sleepily as he continued to stare at my ass.

He shook his head. "You have the prettiest asshole I've ever seen."

If all my blood hadn't made its home in my clit earlier, I would've blushed. As it was, I said, "Um, thanks? I think? That's not a compliment I ever expected to get."

He kissed me again as he gently rubbed my arms and wrists, my legs and ankles, bringing them back to life and getting the circulation to get rid of the pins and needles. "Expect to get all the compliments," he said, and then he was lifting me and carrying me into the bathroom.

After testing the water, he set me down in the shower. He sniffed the shower gel the Airbnb had left for us, shaking his head.

"That bad, huh?" I laughed.

"It doesn't fucking smell like you," he growled. "I don't care if it's made from gold, I only want to smell you when I fuck you."

The flower in my heart unfurled even more, fully in bloom now.

"You sound jealous of a body wash," I teased.

"I am," he growled again. "I'm jealous of every fucking thing that touches you, even if its just soap that doesn't smell right."

His insistence on this, even when he was pissed off and growly, was too sweet.

"What do I smell like?"

He snorted. "Sunshine and sex and some flower I don't know."

"Freesia," I shared helpfully, storing away "sunshine and sex" as three more lovely words he'd said to me.

He shrugged. "Freesia. I'll remember that."

And I knew he was telling the truth. As someone who was always forgotten, having someone remember not just me but the little details felt amazing.

It felt like love.

And when he bent me over in the shower and fucked me again, "just for me this time," I held that thought close to my chest, the sweetest burn I'd ever felt.

After, he held me in bed, face to face, playing with my hair, lost in thought.

But I wanted to talk. So I nudged him.

"Why did you send me away after my parents' funeral?" I asked.

He sighed. "How much do you know about my past?"

"Nothing," I said, pushing at his shoulder. "You're an annoyingly closed book."

"Yeah, okay. See, I never knew my parents. My earliest memories are in foster care. I had no positive parental figures in my life...the closest I came was your dad when I was a teenager. So with no role models, I had no idea how to be a parent to you." He rubbed his forehead. "And just saying that makes me feel really gross, to be clear."

"You aren't my parent," I reminded him gently. "You never even spent time with me during my formative years. But I want to know why."

"Yeah." He sighed again. "I really thought you'd be better off far away from a man like me. I'd been violent when I was younger, used my fists first to protect myself and then as a fucked-up attempt at emotional regulation. The idea of not being in control of that and then having a young kid to care for...what if I screwed up? What if I hurt you? I couldn't risk it, so I sent you away. It didn't occur to me that by abandoning you in your grief, I'd only hurt you more."

I shut my eyes, my heart squeezing in sympathy for this kind, gruff man who was so obsessed with doing the right thing that he always overshot.

"Coach—Blake—listen to me. You could never hurt me physically. All you've done since I came back into your life is protect me. Maybe you didn't always use the most ethical or legal means," I teased. "But you've looked out for me and kept me safe. And it's probably better that I hadn't spent time with you back then, because otherwise we wouldn't be here now."

He shook his head. "No, we'd still be here now. I wouldn't have noticed until you were grown, but there's no alternative reality, no universe exists where I could see you as an adult and not want you as mine. You're it for me, Lucy, I hope you know that." He swallowed. "How the fuck we're going to make this work, I have no idea, but we are."

"Oh, we are," I told him. "Now that I have you, I'm not letting you go. You're mine, Coach Samson, I hope you know that."

"Oh?" he rumbled. "And what are you going to do with me, now that you have me?"

Love you, I thought, but didn't say. I refused to be the one to say it first.

"Oh, I can think of a few things," I teased. "That Vice still working?"

I slid my hand down his chest, his abs, reaching for his hard cock.

And then I slid down after it, taking him in my mouth, showing him how I felt with pleasure since I was too afraid to do it with words.

But when he finished in my mouth and called out my name like the holiest of prayers, I was almost positive he felt the same way, too.

Almost.

30

BLAKE

I could have stayed at that cabin with her forever. Unfortunately, I'd already blown off two days of practice, and Lucy had an organic chemistry exam. So with great reluctance and growing dread at what our life together might look like when we were back in the real world, Lucy and I set the house back to rights—as much as we could. I left a note for our hosts, apologizing for the hole in the wall without explanation, promising to pay for the repairs.

"Ready?" Lucy asked me.

"No," I said truthfully.

"Well, suck it up, buttercup," she told me. "And put your game face on, because we need to go back."

We hadn't discussed what "back" looked like.

We went out to the car and I buckled Lucy in. Maybe it made her feel like a child, but the control it gave me over her safety, knowing she was secure, helped ease some of my anxiety. And she wasn't complaining, especially when I leaned in to kiss her.

The ride back to Tabb was quiet. I drove one handed, the

other on her left thigh, while she gazed out the window. The three hours passed quickly, too quickly, and then we were back, driving through Gehenom past the college bars and bagel shops.

"You should probably drop me off here," Lucy said when we reached the bridge that would take us from College Village into campus. "If you're seen dropping me off at my dorm after we both disappeared for a couple days, people are going to talk."

I wanted to argue with her, to rail against her logic. If I could, I'd drive her straight to the dean's house on the lake and tell him I was dating a student at Tabb who just also happened to be my ward, and he and the board could eat shit if they had a problem with it.

But what good would that do, other than get me fired, Lucy's reputation ruined, and her chances at the pre-vet program destroyed?

I glanced over at her as I pulled to a stop. She was biting her lip, worrying at it, and I brushed my thumb over her mouth and teeth, easing her.

"What's wrong?" I asked gently.

"I think you were right. We should've stayed in that random town," she said. "I'm worried that now that we're back..."

...*you'll go back to treating me like I don't matter*, she didn't have to say.

"Lucy, we're together now," I told her firmly. "This isn't ending because we're back on campus. We'll just have to sneak around for a bit while I figure something out."

"Yeah? Like I'm your naughty little secret?" she teased.

"Something like that," I said.

She looked at me, and I wanted to kiss her, but students were everywhere, on their way to study or drink their

Sunday woes away. I wasn't sure, and I didn't care. I was going to fucking kiss her.

As I leaned in, she stopped me.

"We can't," she said fiercely, and I breathed her in for a moment.

"Don't tell me 'can't,'" I growled, leaning in again.

"Blake, please. Don't do this to us. Not yet."

Damn it.

I fisted my hands, staring at her. "You're mine, Lucy Braverman. I won't kiss you right now and ruin both our lives, if that's what you want, but you're going to make it up to me later. If I have to tie you down spread-eagled to my bed so nothing gets in the way of me kissing you, I will."

She smiled. "You make the sweetest threats, Coach."

And then she was unbuckling her seatbelt, removing my feeling of control over her safety, and hopping out of the car. I watched as she swayed her hips down the bridge pathway, not moving my car until someone behind me honked, before driving home.

♥ ♥

"WHAT THE FUCK?" TREY GREETED ME WHEN I JOINED HIM later that morning in the film study room. I'd gotten home, showered, paced around my house and tried not to go watch the video feed of Lucy's dorm room. I knew she wouldn't be there, but wanted to feel closer to her. Really, I'd had to force myself not to shadow her from class to class to make sure she was safe and no campus douchebag tried to hit on her. I only succeeded because I had to go to work.

"I know, I'm sorry. I had a family emergency," I offered.

It was a pathetic excuse, and Trey knew it.

"You don't have family," he pointed out.

I did, in fact, have family now. Lucy was my family. I may have resisted that for years, but it was true, even if the way she was my family had changed drastically from what I'd ever expected. But if he wasn't picking up on what I actually meant, I wasn't going to explain it to him.

Instead I said, "I'm sorry I wasn't here before, but I'm here now. Our next game is Saturday, so we need to get to work, not sit around and gossip like old women."

Trey looked affronted. "I wasn't fucking gossiping. I was trying to figure out why my *boss* rainchecked a date with my sister, only to disappear for two goddamned days, not respond to a single text, and miss practice. If you lack so much respect for me and this team that you can't even explain where you were, then I have absolutely zero interest working with you anymore."

Ah, shit.

Trey was a great assistant coach; I couldn't lose him.

But I also couldn't tell him what was going on between me and Lucy, not with her entire future and mine in the balance. The stakes had never felt higher, and I still couldn't come up with a solution to our problem.

As my mind raced through lies and I dismissed each one, Trey grew more and more frustrated.

"With all due respect, fuck this," he said, turning toward the door.

As he put his hand on the doorknob, I stopped him, settling for a half-truth.

"When Lucy walked out of the arena that night, she stole my car, drove to a random bar off of Route 13, and was attacked by two men there. I went to get her and took her to the hospital, and I've been with her ever since. I was only looking out for her. She may be eighteen, but I still feel responsible for her."

The bullshit I was sharing tasted sour on my lips. Taking care of Lucy wasn't a responsibility I didn't want, it was an honor I relished. Lying felt cowardly, and as I continued, I felt more and more pathetic.

Trey paused, turning, his face aghast with concern. "Holy shit. Is she okay? Why didn't you respond to my texts and tell me?"

"She didn't want anyone to know." That was likely, and I was going to have to ask Lucy to forgive me.

"Okay." Trey relaxed. I could see it in the way his tight, stiff shoulders loosened, no longer up around his neck. "Well, let's get to work reviewing this game tape and then we can meet the team at practice. Oh, and my sister was asking about you."

I don't want anything to do with your fucking sister. She doesn't hold a goddamned candle to my woman.

But I couldn't say that, or Trey would take offense. Instead I hummed in my throat, found the remote for the big flat screen the university had bought for us, and hit play.

♥‸♥

A COUPLE HOURS LATER, WE STOOD AND STRETCHED, HAVING talked through our notes and feedback for the team based on what we'd seen on the game tape. I checked my watch.

"Emory's still off his game," I observed.

"Yeah. Like I said, he's having woman trouble. I'll talk to him," Trey said.

Was the woman trouble related to Lucy? If so, I was going to have to nip that shit in the bud.

"I'll talk to him," I said.

Trey raised his eyebrow. "You sure?"

I nodded, cracking my knuckles, picturing beating the shit out of Emory if Lucy's name came out of his mouth. "I'm sure."

"All right. We need to head to practice," Trey said, and I agreed.

I was tense on the walk from the film study room down the long hallway to the rink. This was going to be the first time I'd seen Lucy since this morning, and it felt way too fucking long.

Was I going to be able to keep my shit together when she inevitably showed up in a tiny, tight outfit and no bra, knowing my players were ogling every part of her? That Emory was going to see her? Would I be able to stop myself from getting hard remembering what those tits looked like without clothes on, that perfect deep pink pussy, raw and swollen from the number of times I'd made her come with the vibrator?

As we walked, I pulled my phone out of my pocket and sent off a terse text to Lucy.

> Are you still in your dorm?

She responded immediately.

> no, im on my way to practice

> why?

> Turn that hot little ass around and go put on a bra if you aren't already wearing one.

> why?

Why? She was fucking playing with fire, and she knew it.

> Because if you aren't wearing one, I'm going to have to rip out the eyeballs of every other human in the vicinity, and I'd rather not go to jail before the game this weekend.

Instead of responding in the affirmative like a good girl, she sent me a series of kissy lip emojis like the troublemaker she was.

I cracked my knuckles again when we walked into the rink and scanned the large arena. The team was stretching and talking shit, laughing. Lucy was nowhere in the vicinity. Tension filled me, because even if she was late from turning around to put a bra on like I'd ordered, I still needed to see her with my own two eyes. Ever since I'd seen her being held against a wall by those fucking assholes, I'd been hit with the overwhelming need to know where she was at all times. I still wanted to put her in a goddamn collar and attach a leash to her so she was never more than a few feet away from me, forever. I knew that was fucked up, and Lucy would never agree to it, but it didn't make the craving go away.

Finally, she came walking in, swaying her ass, hair up in a high ponytail with pieces curling behind her ears. I immediately relaxed, although seeing her left hand in that brace made me want to beat those assholes to death all over again.

I glanced at her chest and she smirked, tugging down one loose sleeve to expose a lacy black bra strap, before winking at me as she walked over to the players box to grab waters and towels to organize and pass out to the team.

I reached for my phone automatically.

> Pull that sleeve back up, troublemaker.

Feeling her phone vibrate, Lucy pulled it out of her purse, glancing at it. A smile spread across those pink lips and made her shine, brilliant in her beauty.

> and what are you going to do to me if I don't?

Oh, she wanted to play, did she?

> Take it out on your sweet ass.

> promises, promises

I growled under my breath, especially when she tugged her sleeve down even more, exposing even more glowing skin.

Trey tapped my shoulder. "Are you getting sick?"

"No," I said shortly.

"Sure sounds like it," he muttered, but let it go, calling out to Lucy, "You okay, kid?"

Lucy glanced down at her wrist like she'd forgotten all about it.

"Yeah, I'm fine. Just a little accident."

Emory, Mason, and Matt—Emory's roommate—skated up to the box.

"What kind of accident?" Emory asked, sounding concerned—too concerned.

Lucy lifted a shoulder. "Nothing you need to know about."

"Did someone hurt you?" Mason asked, sounding concerned, but in the *you're my fiancée's best friend and so I'm worried because I have to be* way that didn't raise my hackles.

Lucy shut her eyes, and her voice was quiet when she said, "Yeah, just some assholes."

"What the fuck?"

"Where the hell are they?"

"We'll destroy them for you, give us their names."

My team surrounded her, irate, and as territorial as I felt, I couldn't help but be happy that they were so protective of her. Lucy never had that, and as much as I could give that to her, I knew Lucy well enough to know that having other people care so much about her would settle some of the pain inside her chest that her parents had instilled.

Lucy turned her head, glancing over at me, a small, private smile on those lips I needed to take with mine immediately—but wouldn't.

"Coach took care of it," she said, softly but clearly. Her confidence in me settled my annoyance with my team.

"Good," Emory said.

The team echoed their approval, and I blew my whistle and started issuing directions for practice.

I had taken care of it. Just like I'd take care of anything else.

31

LUCY

About ten minutes before practice ended, I excused myself and headed down the tunnel to the locker room. Blake had a smaller office attached to the locker room that he primarily used during games, practices, and to talk to his players individually. I had an idea that excited me, but I needed to get inside his office before the team got there to make sure it happened the way I needed it to.

I entered the empty locker room, bypassing the player's cubbies and the stale sweat smell that pervaded the locker room. Leslie, Tovah, and Aviva had all shared that they'd fucked their guys in the locker room despite the stench, and I wanted to tick that off my Bang Coach Bucket List, or as close to it as possible.

Opening the unlocked door to the office, I crawled under the fortunately tall-enough-to-kneel-under desk and texted Blake.

i'm in your office

He responded immediately.

> What's wrong? Is your wrist hurting? I can
> get you more medication if you need.

His response warmed my chest, filling a hole my parents
had created years ago with their neglect.

> nothing's wrong, i just need my daddy

> Fuck.

> I'm coming.

He was right, he would be soon.

A few minutes later, I heard the door to the locker room
open, the team ribbing each other after practice. The door
to the office squeaked open.

"Lucy?"

Coach sounded confused, clearly unsure where I was.

"Under here, daddy," I called out quietly and sweetly.

"Under where—oh. Oh, fuck," he groaned, figuring out
where I was hiding, and putting together why I was hiding
there immediately.

He joined me behind the desk, sitting in his desk chair
and leaning down to see me.

"Lucy, we could get caught," he told me, but his reluctance was bullshit, given the huge bulge in his pants.

I reached up a hand, stroking over it.

"Not if you're quiet," I teased.

He shut his eyes a moment. "I'm incapable of saying no
to you, which does not bode well for my future."

"I think it bodes very well for your future," I told him,
my hands already working to unbutton and unzip his pants

and release his cock from his boxer briefs. I pulled the thick, gorgeous, hard, and smooth appendage out and wrapped one hand around it, tugging.

His eyes opened, forest green pinning me in place with their intensity.

"Then get to work, sweetheart. Show daddy how good you can make it for him while he does his own job. And then when everyone leaves, he'll take care of you, too."

He always took care of me. It was what I loved most about him, but I wasn't ready to tell him that. No, the words were too scary, too vulnerable, and I refused to say them first in case he didn't say them back. So I'd show him, instead.

He spread his legs wide, allowing me to edge forward on my knees between them. "Use that hot mouth, sweetheart. And play with yourself. But no getting off, no matter how close you are."

"Yes, Coach," I said, opening my mouth and sucking on the tip of his cock, then working my way deeper over it, pleased by his hum of approval as I licked around the crown and the ridge of veins underneath. He'd taught me how he liked it, and I was eager to show him what a good student I was. Obviously, what he liked best was when I took him deep in my throat, but I needed to work my way up to it.

Fortunately, he was being patient with me, because he whispered, "That's right, go slow. Tease me a bit. And touch yourself. Keep your little clit occupied while I deal with a situation."

Then he called out loudly, "Emory, I need to talk to you."

A chorus of "ooohs" echoed through the locker room and made its way into the office. I was curious, but I knew I needed to follow Blake's orders or there would be hell to pay later, even if it was the fun kind of hell.

I slipped a hand inside my leggings and underwear,

stroking my clit. My pussy was already wet, so it was easy, even if I was so sensitive I gasped.

Coach, hearing me, whispered, "shhhhh, sweetheart," and then shunted his hips forward to silence me with even more cock in my mouth, which I sucked on like I had on that dildo the day before.

I heard the squeak of footsteps and then Emory was standing in Blake's office on the other side of the desk.

"Have a seat," Blake offered, and Emory pulled the chair out and sat.

"What's up?" he asked.

"Emory, I respect you too much to ease our way into this conversation. Instead, I'm going to cut straight to the point: Your game has been off lately. I've noticed, Trey has noticed, even your teammates have noticed. You're not focused, you miss easy shots, your stick work is sloppy, and your head is clearly elsewhere. Trey told me it's girl problems. Is that true?"

Emory sighed. "Fuck. Yeah, it is. I'm not going to tell you—"

"Is it Lucy?" Blake interrupted.

Wait, what?

I popped my mouth off Blake's cock, surprised. Why the hell would Blake think I was the girl in Emory's life? Sure, I'd flirted with him, but I flirted with everyone but Mason to make Blake jealous. Had he not seen through that? I knew I'd been playing with fire at the last game by wearing Emory's jersey, but I assumed that Blake now understood it hadn't meant anything. I didn't want Emory to get shit because of my own games.

As I considered how to handle this situation without exposing us to Emory, Blake reached under the desk, gripping my head and forcing me back onto his cock...deep on his cock. So deep, I almost gagged. His point was clear. I didn't get to stop; he was in charge—in both this conversation and of my mouth. I swallowed around him to ease the pressure on my throat, and Blake repeated, "You heard me. Is it Lucy?"

The aggression in his tone wasn't hidden at all. What the hell was he doing?

Emory laughed in shock. "Luc— no, it's not Lucy. Lucy and I joke around, but I've never been remotely interested in her. I'm not into blondes." He hesitated, then added, "Or younger women, for that matter."

"Oh," Blake said, relief evident in his voice.

He settled, his cock retreating a bit from my mouth, giving me more space to breathe. I took the opportunity, settling as well.

Then Blake, observant as ever, lit on, "Older women?"

Emory sighed. "Yeah, Coach. It's fucked, I know, and I can't have her. I've never wanted someone like this before in my life. I can't distract myself from thinking about her. She plagues every thought in my head. I close my eyes at night, I see her. I breathe, I smell her. I eat, I wonder what her pussy tastes like...ah, sorry, that's probably TMI."

Blake chuckled. "It's fine."

Relieved, Emory continued, spilling out everything like he couldn't control himself. "I know I'm off my game. I'm motherfucking *obsessed*, and it's messing me up. My grades are terrible except for in my intro to lit class..."

Oh, wow.

Emory was exposing way too much information, although Blake was trustworthy.

"I don't know what the hell to do."

Blake was quiet for a second, although his body was active. His hips shifted forward and back as he thrust into my mouth—then retreated, thrusting into my mouth, then retreated again. Filling me this way, his complete control over the conversation and me, made my thighs go tight. I worked my clit slowly, edging myself, but witnessing his complete and utter competence and confidence made it hard not to give in and let myself come.

Especially when he asked, "Is she married?"

"No," Emory said, although then he added, "Not that I'd give a fuck if she was."

"Then my only suggestion is to make it happen. I know from experience that if you try to ignore or suppress those feelings, it only makes everything worse. The only thing that helps is to claim what you want, show her you're in charge, and do everything in your power to lock her down and keep her. Whatever that means, do it. We need you at 100 percent, so do what you have to do to get there. Trust me, once she's yours completely, and you know she's not going anywhere, you'll be able to get your head back on straight."

My heart stuttered in my chest at the sincerity behind his words, my fingers working faster despite myself, mouth eagerly working back and forth as I licked and sucked and swallowed around him in approval and gratitude. Hearing the truth about how he felt, even if he didn't say he loved me, was exactly what I needed to hear.

"Got it, Coach," Emory said, his chair squeaking as he stood. And then he said, "Take good care of Lucy, okay? She needs it."

Blake said nothing for a moment, clearly as floored as I was that Emory had a hunch about what was going on. Then he said, "I promise I will to my dying day. But Emory..."

"Stays between us. Doesn't need to be said," Emory

replied, and then I heard his footsteps and the door shutting softly behind him.

"Fuck," Blake exhaled, and I wasn't sure if it was out of pleasure or relief.

I pulled off his cock to say, "Are we in trouble?"

Blake coughed. "We aren't, but you are. Did I say you could stop? Get that mouth back to work. I want in that tight little throat."

Reaching down, he grabbed my head again, pulling me back onto his cock, forcing my head over it, more and more, until his cock edged down into my throat and my nose was pushed up against his skin.

"How close are you?" he asked.

I moaned, since I couldn't speak.

"That close, huh?" he said knowingly. "Okay, stop playing with your pussy and play with my balls instead. Everyone's leaving and I want to come down that tight little..."

He trailed off as the door to his office opened again, and there was the clack of...

...high heels on tile.

What the hell?

Blake didn't release my head but didn't move his hips either, holding me tight as I fought to breathe through my nose as he asked politely, "Can I help you?"

"I certainly hope so," Professor Putrovski trilled. "You never called or texted, but I'm a modern woman who knows what she wants, so I decided to take fate in my own hands and come ask you out."

"Oh, shit," Blake said under his breath, retreating from my mouth a bit.

Oh, shit was right. I was confident he didn't want her; he'd made that clear. But how was he going to get out of this? What if he didn't? What if protecting my future and his was more important to him?

Determined, I leaned in and worked his cock deeper into my mouth, swallowing again until it slid back into my mouth.

"Oh, shit," Blake said again, this time less quietly.

"Excuse me?" my professor asked, confused.

"My apologies," Blake said smoothly. "Was just remembering something I forgot to do."

"Well, I won't keep you long," Professor Putrovksi said stiffly. This clearly wasn't going the way she'd expected, or hoped. "There's the alumni gala on Thursday, and I thought we could go together."

Oh, this bitch. Maybe I had no real reason to think of her as a bitch, but she was, regardless. I hollowed out my cheeks around Blake's cock, swallowing around him as I reached a hand underneath him and circled his taint.

"Yeahhhhhhh," Blake groaned despite himself, slapping a hand on the desk. It was obvious the yeah was to me and not her, but the professor had no way of knowing, damn it.

"Yes?" she asked, sounding happy.

"Yeah, no. I can't. I already have a commitment that night."

"A commitment to something other than the alumni dinner where donors give money to the hockey team you're in charge of?" she asked sharply.

"A commitment to someone else," he said succinctly as he surged deeper into my mouth, if that was even possible, choking me.

I gurgled unintentionally, cursing myself in case she could hear. Although maybe she should hear. Maybe if she knew there was someone underneath his desk, that *I* was underneath his desk, she'd give up on trying to date *my* man. Coach was mine, no one else could have him.

"Oh? Who?"

Blake didn't answer her for a moment as he stroked my cheek.

"Someone immensely important to me. The most important. I'm sorry, Alex."

"Alison," she snapped.

"I'm sorry, Alison. I'm not the man for you. I wish you the best of luck. Now, I have to get back to that project I'd forgotten, but hope you'll come to our games later in the season. Take care of yourself."

He dismissed her, and I cheered in my head.

But clearly she needed a parting shot, because she said, "You should tell your ward when you next see her that I'm reconsidering her recommendation letter. Her behavior lately has made it clear her priorities are skewed, and she's not right for the program."

I froze, forgetting to breathe—and not because of the way Blake's cock was taking up every available millimeter in my mouth. Would she really take that away from me because she had guessed what I meant to Blake, or even as a threat to get him to date her? What a fucking bitch! What was I going to do?

As if sensing my worry, Coach stroked my hair again.

"Alison," he said, his voice calm and terrifying. "You and I both know that Lucy deserves to be in that program. If you renege on your promise to write her a recommendation letter out of some tantrum because I'm not interested in you, I'll destroy your life. You're going to want to reconsider your decision, I promise you that. You may not get me as a partner, but you certainly don't want me for an enemy."

The professor didn't say a word, clacking out of the office. A moment later, the door slammed.

Coach sighed, rolling back in his chair as he pulled out of my mouth, leaving me gasping for air.

He reached down, dragging me out from the desk, standing and lifting to sit me on it so I faced him, face flushed and hair a mess. I glanced down at his cock, hard and thick, slapping his stomach, almost purple from not having come yet.

"She's going to fuck everything up for us," I blurted out as I raised my head to stare up at him.

He shook his head. "She won't."

"She will," I insisted.

"No, she won't," he said, kneeling down in front of me as he pulled down my leggings and panties so they dangled around my calves, then shoving me down on the desk. "I said I'll take care of it, and I will. You're not going to lose out on anything you want, as long as I'm on this earth. Don't worry about that right now—worry about how hard I'm about to make you come."

"But—" I started.

He cut me off as he latched his mouth onto my clit and sucked, hard. I shrieked, and this time he didn't bother to silence me, just sucked harder, the pressure so intense my back bowed and I shrieked again.

"Blake!"

"That's not what you fucking call me," he practically snapped, then bit—actually *bit*—my clit in reprimand.

"Daddy!" I screamed that time as I came from the combination of sharp pain and aching pleasure.

He lifted his head, pulling the coach whistle off his neck, and as I came, I watched as he shoved the cold metal directly into my pussy, using it to push against my g-spot, then leaning down to suck my clit into his mouth again. The combination of the cold pressure of the whistle against my insides and his mouth against my outsides shot me into the stratosphere, especially when he began to move it inside me. I cried, actually sobbed, as a tightness I hadn't even been aware of released and liquid leaked out of me. Shit. Had I peed?

"Ah fuck, you squirted all over my whistle," Blake groaned, and then he was pulling it out of me and thrusting his tongue into me, licking up and out all my cum, like he needed to drown in my taste.

His greedy, relentless mouth took no prisoners and didn't give me a break, forcing me to come again from the unending pleasure.

"Why? Why did you do that?" I finally gasped.

"Because I wanted you to feel good," he said, releasing my pussy and rising to his feet. "But mostly because now I'll be able to smell your sweet cunt at every fucking practice and game. Taste you every time I use it to get those jackass players in order. A constant reminder that you're mine, Lucy Braverman."

Then he was gripping my hip with one hand, pulling me down on the desk and gripping his cock with the other, shoving inside so deep, I felt him everywhere, my chest, my stomach, my throat. He powered his hips against me, again and again, a slapping sound taking over the small office as he fucked me and fucked me and fucked me, hurting me so good as he roared my name and came, filling me up so full with him I had no choice but to come with him.

He kept me busy for a while, until I forgot about the professor and my fears, showing me with his body that I could trust him to handle things.

And so I did.

32

LUCY

T hings seemed to calm down a bit after that. Between classes, studying, practice, and sneaking around with Blake, the next couple days were too busy for me to worry about Professor Putrovski. In class, she was especially cold with me, but didn't go out of her way to embarrass me or make me look bad, so I decided she had listened to Coach's threat and let it go.

Coach and I fucked all the time, in his home office, his office in the arena, in the locker room, even in a utilities closet at the arena one late night, only to be almost caught by a janitor. Every night, he'd pick me up and take me to his house, where we'd fuck some more, and then he'd hold me all night, murmuring to me about how much he cared. He never said he loved me, though, so I never said it, either.

The day before the gala, he handed me his credit card and told me to go out and buy a stunning dress.

"For what?" I asked.

"For the alumni dinner, obviously," he said. "You're going as my date."

I gaped at him. "I'm going as your *what*?"

"My date."

"I'm sorry, did I miss something? Did they change university policy about professors and staff fraternizing with undergraduates?" I asked in shock, and if I was honest, excitement.

"We can play it off as me bringing you as my ward, but I want you there. In a gorgeous dress. So take my credit card and go get one."

I decided not to point out to him that I had plenty of money to go buy my own dress. I had no idea how he was planning on pulling this off, but if he thought he could, I'd believe him.

I took Leslie to Pixie, a size-inclusive boutique in town, one of the few stores that sold dresses that would actually fit my large breasts, trying on and discarding dress after dress until I found the perfect one. It was all black and seemed demure from the front, with a high neckline and a long, straight skirt. But when I turned around, my back was entirely bare, all the way to right above my ass. Blake would lose his mind over it— I couldn't wait. The dress was thousands of dollars, and I considered paying for it myself, but Blake called me while I was in the dressing room and reminded me to use his card.

"If you don't, I won't let you come for a goddamn month," he warned.

I didn't like the sound of that, so I used his card.

The next night, I stood in Blake's bedroom, eyeing myself critically.

"Red lipstick or pink?" I called where he was shaving in the bathroom.

The sound of the electric razor stopped, and he peeked his head out.

"Pink—ah fuck, look at all that bare skin," he growled, coming to stand behind me and wrapping his arm around my waist under my breasts, tugging me tight against him. "You're fucking stunning, and we'll be lucky if I don't end up beating someone up for looking at you."

"You can't," I told him, a little breathless from how gorgeous he looked in his tux, freshly shaved. I was captivated by how good we looked together, his short, dark hair and green eyes contrasting sharply but harmoniously with my blonde waves and brown eyes.

He nodded, his eyes on fire. "You're right. But we're going to be late, so I'm soothed by knowing my cum will be inside you the whole time."

"We're going to be late," I told him.

"I don't care. Bend over, sweetheart."

I did, pressing my right hand against the mirror, balancing as well as I could with a brace still on my left wrist. Blake unzipped his pants, lifted my dress, shoved my panties to the side, and fucked me hard and fast, watching me through the mirror through the entire time, eyes intense on mine until we both came.

♥ ♥
▲

WHEN WE WALKED INTO THE ALUMNI DINNER, CONSPICUOUSLY late, we drew everyone's attention. Alumni, board members, and hockey players were dressed in black tie, sitting laughing at tables covered in white linen with large candelabras. The laughter died as they saw us. Blake's hand had been resting on my back, but I moved away from him, aware of people's eyes, their shocked whispers. In the corner,

Professor Putrovski sat next to Trey, her disapproving glare trained on me.

Based on the fact that Trey was sitting next to her, that was our table.

"I changed my mind," I murmured. "Let's go back home. This is too much."

Dimly, I was aware I'd called his house "home," and tried not to recoil at how that must have sounded to him, like I'd just assumed it was ours when he'd never—

Blake moved next to me, whispering in my ear. "The only word I heard you say was *home.* Because you're right, it is home. *Our* home."

Oh.

Well.

I straightened my shoulders. If Blake considered his house ours, then who was I to argue?

Tossing my hair, I said, "Let's do this."

Standing tall, I made my way over to the table in the back corner, doing my best not to let my professor's cold stare affect me. I took comfort in Blake's warm, solid presence behind me. When we reached the table, Blake pulled out a chair, which I sat in as gracefully as possible, a smile glued to my face. He pulled out the chair next to mine, sitting in it close to me so that his thigh pressed against mine. It was a reminder, we were a team, he had my back, and I didn't have to worry because he'd take care of everything. It was hard to believe it, especially when Trey raised an eyebrow and said, "Interesting choice of date."

"I wanted to bring someone important to me, and Lucy's important to me," he said simply.

"Well, she is your ward," Trey said, trying to dispel the awkwardness.

"That's not why I brought her," Blake said.

The professor said nothing, but her pursed lips said everything.

I opened my mouth to say something, also wanting to break the ice, but Blake squeezed my thigh under the table, and I shut it.

The four of us were silent as waiters placed salads in front of us. Blake flagged one down before they walked away.

"She's allergic to carrots," he said. "Please go make her a salad with no carrots, and make sure it hasn't touched carrots."

He knew about my allergy? Although I guess he did have that dossier on me.

As if he sensed my surprise, he said, "I know everything about you, Lucy. Everything." He said it loudly, his eyes trained on Trey and his sister, as if daring them to say anything. Neither did, although the professor's face looked even more sour.

They still didn't say anything when the waiter brought me a salad, and Blake began to eat. I ate too, calmed slightly by the feeling of his hand on my thigh, and the knowledge that I still had his cum inside me.

The people across the table from us, unaware of the tension, tried to draw us into conversation. Blake chatted and joked with them easily, and usually I would have too, but I was too deep in my emotion and wonder. I loved the way he took care of me, the way he knew me, from the big things to the little details, to his solidness and steadiness and control. I especially loved the way I could make his control snap. I loved him so much, and I wanted—no, *needed* —to tell him. Even if he didn't say it back, I was going to be brave, because I was always brave. I wasn't hiding from it anymore, and if he broke my heart...well, better now than later.

But first I needed to pee and then psych myself up.

I excused myself from the table, Coach's eyes trailing me, a concerned question sharpening their deep green color. I waved him off and walked out of the ballroom, steeling myself against the whispers. Coach and I had made an entrance, after all, and while some people might wave it away as a kind thing he'd done for his legal ward, others may have sensed the sexual tension between us, seen the way he'd placed his hand on my back, and made other, more accurate assumptions.

In the bathroom, a lavish affair with plush seating and ornate gold bordered mirrors, I peed, a little mystified by just how much of Coach's cum had dried between my thighs. I really should have been grossed out, but instead it filled me with pride. I felt claimed, felt *owned* in a hot, safe, and perfect way, and I was going to cling to that feeling as I told him how I felt.

After finishing up, I flushed and went to go wash my hands, rehearsing the "Blake, I love you" in my head when someone joined me at the sinks. Glancing in the mirror, I froze, my professor's harsh glare staring back at me.

"You look lovely," I offered, because what the fuck else was I supposed to say?

"You look like jailbait," she said.

My mouth fell open.

"Big, perky tits, long blonde hair, longer legs...no wonder he wants you. A lot of men would turn into animals when it comes to a hot eighteen-year-old willing to spread her thighs for the slightest hint of affection. Girls with daddy issues." She tsked. "Men fall for it every time."

My teeth were clenched so tight, my jaw hurt. "Do you have a point?"

She laughed, cruel and wicked. "They fall for it...at first. But see, while they may be attracted to youth, they get bored quickly. At the end of the day, they want a partner who can match them, hold a conversation with them. Make them laugh. Let me give you some advice from experience you're too young to have had yourself. Being a slut only gets you so far in life, and the man or men you're a slut for now will disappear later, leaving you with nothing."

She grinned at herself, satisfied.

"Professor, thank you," I said.

She turned to me, confused, expecting...I don't know what, tears? "For?"

"For giving me an excuse to do this," I said, and then, fisting my right hand like I'd seen Coach do, with my thumb on the outside to protect it, I slung it in her direction, punching her directly in the nose.

She screamed. It was really satisfying, although not as satisfying as the blood dripping down her nose, pooling at her chin, making her pretty face look macabre, and well... not quite so pretty. Honestly, it made up for how fucking much my right hand hurt, and it hurt a lot...worse than my left wrist, which was still in its brace. I'd never punched another woman in my life, but she'd fucking deserved it, and I felt not even a speck of remorse.

Shaking out my hand, I turned to leave, ignoring her pained, shocked cries as she covered her bleeding nose with her hand. Then, I stopped and turned back to face the mirror, catching her glance.

"Professor? You're a real cunt. I honestly hope you learn how not to be, or you're going to be alone for a very, very long time. You can take your intercollegiate veterinary program and shove it up your ass next to the stick there. I bet it's the most action you'll get."

With that, I blew a kiss at the mirror and left her crying in the bathroom, making my way back to the ballroom. I had a man to tell that I loved him, after all.

33

BLAKE

I sat at the table with Trey, silently worrying. Lucy had gone to the bathroom, seeming stressed, and then Trey's sister, whose name I had forgotten again, had excused herself to the bathroom as well. I wanted to go after her, because god only knew what she would say to Lucy, but I had no real excuse to leave.

Well, except to go to the bathroom myself.

"I'll be right back," I said.

"Don't," Trey said flatly. "It's obvious you're fucking her, and I want to know what your plan is here. Because you know they'll fire you as soon as they find out, and the entire board is here, so I'm pretty sure they know."

I shrugged. "My only plan is to be with her."

He snorted. "Well, thanks for fucking over the entire team."

In the past, that would've stopped me in my tracks. I was responsible to my team, and my team alone. But now, all that responsibility meant nothing. My priority was Lucy, and Lucy alone. If that meant I had to quit, if we both had to transfer to another university with a good pre-vet program, then so be it. I'd sell my house, pack us both up, and leave tomorrow.

As if reading my mind, Trey asked, "What about playoffs?"

"You're a good coach," I told him. "A great one. You can see them through."

Saying that hurt my chest, but nowhere near what giving Lucy up would.

He blinked. "Is she really worth it?"

"And more," I said easily. "She's worth every goddamn sacrifice in the whole fucking world, even my life if it came down to that. One day you'll get that, Trey. You'll meet a woman who flips your whole world upside down, until all that matters is her happiness. One day, you'll feel about someone the way I feel about Lucy. One day you'll lo—"

There was a tap on my shoulder.

I turned my head to look at Lucy, bright eyed, blushing, and oh so beautiful, smelling of sex and sunshine.

Had she heard me? Maybe she had. It was time to tell her how I felt, after all. And if that meant finding out she actually didn't feel the same way...well, better to know that now so I could set her free, even if I doubted my ability to let her go.

No, I'd lock her away forever and force her to love me before I could make that happen.

"Come dance with me," she said, holding out her good hand.

A hand with red knuckles.

"What the—"

"Come dance with me," she repeated, reaching for my hand. "Please."

At her *please*, I rose, following her onto the dance floor.

Even though the band was playing—an instrumental version of Hozier's "Work Song,"—no one else was on the dance floor. But if this was what Lucy wanted, this is what she would have.

I pulled her into my arms, not bothering to keep things appropriate for the people watching, holding her tight as we swayed to the music. I looked down at her, grabbing her right hand and inspecting it.

Raw, angry knuckles.

With blood on them.

"Lucy," I asked. "What the hell happened to your hand? Who do I have to kill?"

"I don't think you have to kill anyone," she said, but her voice was shaky. "I'm pretty sure I took care of it."

Warning bells went off in my head.

"Lucy," I warned. "Tell me right now."

"Um..." she trailed off. "Professor Putrovski may have called me a slut a few times—"

"What?!"

"—And I may have punched her in the nose," Lucy finished, looking up at me like she expected me to get mad at her. "Whoops?" she finished, offering me a questioning smile.

Her words sank in.

That bitch had called her a slut.

And Lucy had hauled off and punched her in the face.

I threw back my head and laughed, because only my troublemaker would do such a perfectly wild thing.

She watched me, biting her lip. Around us, people began to murmur, wondering why I was laughing so hard, but I couldn't stop, practically wheezing from how fucking funny it was.

Finally, I calmed.

"Good for you," I said. "I'm glad you punched her, so I didn't have to. Is it her blood, or yours?"

She grinned at me. "Hers."

Still holding her hand, I gazed down at Lucy as I lifted it to my lips, kissing each knuckle one at a time, aware I was getting blood on my lips and not caring.

Leaning down close, I whispered to her. "Your badassedness is only one reason I'm in love with you, little troublemaker."

Her lips formed an O. An O I wanted my cock to slide deep into, but there'd be time for that later. First, I needed to share how I felt, even if it killed me.

"You're in—"

"I'm in love with you," I confirmed, heart in my throat. "I love you. I love your strength, I love your sass, I love how fucking smart you are, I love your body and your mind, but mostly, I love how big your heart is. How you love animals as well as people, and how you love yourself, with this unwavering bravery that's honestly inspiring. I love every fucking thing about you, and even if you don't love me back, I'm not letting you go. Lie, cheat, or steal, even kill. You're mine, Lucy Samson, and I'm yours," I said, intentionally giving her my last name. "We belong to each other until the day I fucking die, and after that, too."

I stood there, having figuratively ripped my heart out of my chest and placing it into her delicate hands, waiting for the worst, hoping for the best. She could drop it on the ground and smash it with her foot, or she could hold it close for me. It was out of my control now, and shockingly, it felt good.

I didn't have to wait long, because Lucy was flinging her arms around my waist, saying, "I love you, Blake Samson. I'm not letting you go, either. I've loved you since

I was a little girl. I've just been waiting for you to catch up."

In that moment, I decided I didn't give a shit about the people around us, or all the explaining I was about to have to do—not only about the fact that I was going to marry a student but marry my legal ward, at that. I didn't care about the scandal about to befall us, I needed Lucy more. Wrapping a hand around her head, I leaned down and kissed her hard, forcing her to open her mouth under mine and diving in with my tongue, forgetting everything but the taste, the smell, and the feel of her. She loved me. She *loved* me. She was fucking mine, forever, and I wouldn't have to lock her away to keep her, I could just keep her. For once in my life, someone belonged to me, and I belonged to someone else. Our two broken souls had somehow found each other, and I thanked whatever fucking entity that had made this possible, because I was never, ever, letting her go.

I would have kept kissing her, until I heard a woman yelling something angrily. Pulling away from Lucy's perfect mouth, I looked over her shoulder, where Trey's sister stood, one hand over her bleeding nose, with rage-filled eyes.

Next to her stood the president of the university, Saul Glazer.

And a cop.

Oh, fuck.

"That fucking bitch punched me in the nose!" she squawked.

The music stopped. Gasps echoed in the big ballroom.

"Who the hell are you calling a bitch?" I said as I shoved Lucy behind me, facing the professor with her now messed up face.

"Your little slut," she sneered.

I stepped forward.

So did Saul.

I turned to him. "Are you really going to let a faculty member speak to a young student that way?"

He winced. "I don't love her language, but I like a student assaulting a faculty member even less."

THE COP WAS HOLDING OUT HANDCUFFS, CLEARLY MEANT FOR Lucy. So I immediately dismissed the professor and Saul, turning to him instead.

"Don't you come near her," I warned. "You even think about it, and you'll have to haul me in, too."

"Then I'll have to haul you in," the officer said solemnly. "Because—"

"Because I'm pressing charges," the professor spat. "And when I'm done with her, she won't be a student at Tabb anymore. She won't be a student *anywhere*."

Rage burned through me, and it was only Lucy tugging on the back of my tux jacket that kept me from grabbing the professor by the throat, woman or not. I was going to destroy her if she even tried to hurt Lucy. I'd meant that before, and I meant it now.

"Unfortunately, we'll need to bring her into the station to get a statement," the officer said, clearly uncomfortable to be in the middle of all this drama. "You're welcome to follow us there, but she'll have to come in the back of my car—"

"Then I'm coming with you," I told him flatly. "Lucy goes nowhere without me."

More gasps.

"That's not how that works, unless we're arresting you, too…"

Taking three steps forward, I once again faced the president of the university—the university where I worked, the one that paid each and every one of my bills.

And punched him in the face to a chorus of gasps.

The gasps in the ballroom turned into screams, as Saul stumbled to his feet, blood trickling from his mouth.

"Blake, what the hell did you do?" Lucy asked, trembling.

"Don't worry, sweetheart, it'll all be okay," I promised.

"Arrest him, too," Saul said, disappointment in his eyes as he spat out blood. "Blake, I don't know what's gotten into you, but between getting involved with a student you never should have touched, and becoming violent to protect her, you aren't the man I thought you were."

"You're right," I said. "I'm better. *She* makes me better."

It was true. I'd fought so long and so hard against losing control, I hadn't realized what I'd gained. I'd give up everything else if it meant keeping Lucy by my side, safe and happy.

So I was glad when the cop, only having one set of handcuffs, used them on me instead of her before marching us both out of the ballroom and the building, directly into the back of his car. At least we got to ride together, Lucy leaning her head against my shoulder, as we prepared to face what came next.

♥⸰♥

THEY SEPARATED US AT THE STATION, BUT THEY GAVE ME MY one phone call. I immediately called Micah, telling him I needed a favor from his brother Marcus.

"He'll say you owe him one," Micah warned. "And he always, always makes you pay."

But I didn't care, so he said he'd take care of it.

A few hours later, after pacing back and forth in lockup, worrying about Lucy and losing my shit that I couldn't get to her, an officer appeared, opening the metal barred door.

"Your lawyer's here," he said stiffly, and I followed him out, down the hall, into a small dark room.

"Where the hell is Lucy Braverman?" I asked.

He didn't answer, just left me there.

Moments later, a woman and man entered the room, the woman holding a briefcase, the man an easy smirk—the kind of a smirk you only smiled if you were worth billions of dollars and had nothing to worry about, ever.

That was Marcus, which meant the woman must be—

"Ilana Brandeis," she said formally. "And before you ask, I've already seen Lucy. She's fine."

Relieved, I sat in the chair. "Thank you."

She waved me off. "I know how you men are by now. If I hadn't handled her case first, you'd be barking at me to go do it."

She was right.

She also got right to work.

"Here's the deal," she said. "Marcus and Micah were able to find dirt on Professor Alison Putrovski, and they...spoke to her. Micah looked into her, and it turns out she lied about graduating from her Ph.D. program. She never should have gotten this job in the first place. It took a little leaning on her, but she dropped the charges against Lucy, and will still write a recommendation for some program Lucy's interested in."

Oh, thank fuck.

"You, however, punched your university president, and although I can protect you legally, there's very little I can do to protect your job. Marcus is willing to bail you out, but this will go on your record, and Saul Glazer is unwilling to let you stay on at the university."

Once upon a time, losing my coaching job would have destroyed me. Now...I shrugged. "I doubted I was keeping my job anyway once my relationship with Lucy became public." She was more important than any job. "Am I going to have to go to prison?"

"No." Ilana grinned like a shark. "I was able to work him down from that. But you will have to pay a very, very hefty fine...and it's going to be difficult to find another coaching job."

"Which is where I come in," Marcus said, smoothing nonexistent lint off his suit jacket. "I'll pay the fine, so you don't have to worry about it. But I'll need a favor."

Ah, here we go.

"Yes?"

"As it turns out, I am deeply in need of a head coach with your talents. You see, I recently purchased an NHL team here in Gehenom, The Beasts, and the coach is...well, let's just say he's subpar. If you're interested in the job, we'll make all this go away. If you aren't...well, I guess you'll have to enjoy prison...and unemployment."

Ilana chuckled. "Well, until Lucy comes into her trust in a few years."

I glowered. Fuck that. I was going to provide for Lucy, not the other way around. She could use the money from her inheritance to start an animal sanctuary for every stray in the world, for all I cared.

Besides. This was a dream.

Head coach of an NHL team? My former NHL team?

"What's the catch?" I asked.

Marcus's smirk widened into a smile. "The catch is you have to trade four of the players for my little brother and his three friends. You see, my brother doesn't always make the best choices, and this will allow me to keep a closer eye on him."

Ah.

Family drama.

Well, it wasn't my problem.

I held out my hand, cracked and blood-dried knuckles and all.

"Deal," I said.

"Deal," Marcus repeated, and although I felt like I'd signed on with the devil, I wasn't going to worry about it.

We were in Gehenom, after all.

"Now, let me see Lucy," I said immediately.

"Of course, you're free to go. She's waiting outside."

I couldn't have gotten out of there sooner. The police gave me back my things, grumbling about shady dealings with shadier lawyers, and then I was out of the precinct and on the street in the early morning light.

Lucy sat on the steps, tapping away on her phone.

"Lucy, sweetheart," I rasped, storming down the stairs toward her, lifting her up and spinning her around so she was in my arms.

I searched her. Her hair was a little mussed up, and there was some dirt on her dress, but otherwise, she was no worse for wear.

"You okay?" I asked her.

"Am I okay? Are *you* okay? What the hell were you thinking, hitting *the president of Tabb* like that?"

Well, that was easy. I set her down but gripped her upper arms to keep her close.

"I was thinking if I hit him, he'd press charges and the police would be forced to take me in the cop car with you. And I didn't want to be away from you for a single second.

I'm fine, in fact, I think we're actually both going to be fine. I told you I'd handle it, didn't I?"

She laughed, and the relieved sound lit up my chest like sparkling wine, making me feel fucking giddy. Me, Coach Samson, the grumpiest fucker alive, giddy.

"You did, although this was not what I figured 'handling it' meant."

I shrugged. "I'd do anything for you. I will do anything for you. You know that, right? You're the most important thing in the world to me. I love you."

"I love you, too," she said, rising onto her toes to kiss me. "Let's go home."

Home.

Our home.

"Yeah, sweetheart, let's go home," I said, even though for me, home was wherever she was. Although our actual home had restraints under the bed, restraints I had plans for.

"You know," she said, as we waited for Marcus to join us and drive us home, "when I pictured being handcuffed, that wasn't what I had in mind."

I growled.

"Fortunately, I have the perfect handcuffs for a trouble-maker like you," I said. "We can use them when we get home."

"Promise?" she asked, eyes brilliant with lust and affection.

"Promise," I said, because I'd give her whatever she wanted. And if what she wanted was to be restrained with handcuffs and a spreader bar while I fucked her in half, well, then that's exactly what I'd do.

Because for her, I'd do anything.

"I love you, troublemaker," I said. "I'm not the most eloquent of men, and I wish I had the right words to make it clear just how important you are to me. Because you *are* the most important thing that exists. I used to fear losing control, but if losing control means gaining you in the process, then it was motherfucking worth it. I can't promise I'll ever find the right words, and I won't promise that I won't keep you under lock and key to keep you safe and mine. But I do promise I'll show you how much I love you, every goddamn day for the rest of our lives."

Her eyes filled with tears, the happy kind.

"I love you, too, Blake Samson. And you can start by kissing me."

So I did. She was the first woman in my life I'd kissed, and she'd be the last. And that made me the luckiest fucker in the world.

"Let's go home," she said against my lips.

And we did.

EPILOGUE
LUCY

Some Months Later

"**G**ood work today, Lucy," my animal behavior professor at Reina said to me as we filed out of class. "Professor Putrovski was right; you're a great addition to the program."

At Professor Putrovski's name, I winced. Since she hadn't had tenure, she'd left Tabb under less than auspicious circumstances, and I was one of the few people who knew why. But before she'd left, she'd written me the recommendation letter she'd promised, which had been the last thing I needed to get into the pre-vet program I'd been dreaming about. So far, the classes had been excellent, and it looked like vet school—and my future—were within reach.

"Thank you," I told my new professor. I glanced at my phone. "I have somewhere to be, so I'll see you tomorrow!"

I headed out to the parking lot, getting in the car Coach had bought me. I'd pointed out to him that I had a substantial inheritance, but then he'd told me he was paying so I let it go, donating the money I would've spent on a car to a local animal shelter. I put on Sabrina, singing along as I drove off campus and through the city until I reached the Gehenom Beasts' arena, parking in my usual spot before heading into the building.

It was a space I knew well from my childhood, but now, as the girlfriend of their head coach, it had new meaning. Some people treated us strangely when they figured out our original relationship, but I brushed it off. After all, I was someone who was made for scandal, and seeing people's shocked looks and hearing their whispers made me laugh. Like Blake said, I was trouble, and by being with him and flaunting our relationship publicly, all I was doing was living the promise of the nickname he'd given me.

Heading down the hall, I knocked on his office door.

When he opened it, he was on the phone. I went to wait on the couch, but he shook his head.

"Hold on one second," he told whoever he was speaking to, covering the speaker.

"Strip," he told me.

Watching me, he continued his conversation—something about a trade—raising an eyebrow as I hesitated.

His eyes grew hard, and he walked up to me, still talking on the phone as he ripped my dress open, buttons flying everywhere.

Not wanting him to do the same to my bra, because finding bras in my size was practically impossible, I quickly opened the clasp and slid it off, along with my destroyed dress and my panties, until I was standing there, naked except for my heels.

Coach's green eyes darkened with desire as he looked me over, and I shivered. We must have fucked hundreds of times by now, but every time he saw me, he had the same look of desperate, out of control worship that he'd had the first time. He'd called me a miracle a few times, and after a while, I had no choice but to believe him.

He pointed at his desk, and I walked toward it and waited like a good girl, until he circled his finger a few times, signaling that he wanted me to face it. As I did, he pushed down on my naked back, sending shivers through me as he forced me to bend over the desk.

"Handle it," he told whoever it was on the phone, and hung up.

"Ah fuck, sweetheart, you look so pretty like that," he said, bending over and placing a kiss on my spine, sending even more shivers everywhere.

I squirmed.

He tapped my inner thigh.

"Spread your legs," he demanded, and I did.

Satisfied, he opened the drawer, pulling a few things out of it, closing it again, and then walking around behind it, placing the items out of eyesight.

"You know what would look even prettier, Lucy?"

"What?" I asked, a little breathless as he stroked a hand over my hip.

"My cock up that tight little ass," he said, tone serious, and I heard the pop of a tube being opened. Cold gel was spread over my opening in circles before Blake pushed it inside with his fingers.

I forced myself to relax. We'd played enough with butt plugs and fingers that I knew it would hurt more if I was tense. We'd never done this, but I wanted to. I wanted to do everything with him.

"Good, good girl," he praised in a low voice as he fucked one finger into my ass, then two, squeezing out more lube from the tube and working it generously into my tight hole. I heard one more squeeze, and then a zipper, and then, the best sound of all, the wet sound of a lubed hand working over his thick, hard cock.

"We're going to see if you can come just from this," Blake said. "Usually I'd get you off by playing with your pussy, but you're such a good girl, I bet you can have an anal orgasm for daddy, can't you?"

His words, exciting and terrifying, made me clench.

"Yeah, sweetheart, that's right," he said, picking up on it. "Now, relax, release your breath, and bear down."

I did as he said, and then his cock was right there at my entrance, making me jump from the tingly feeling of him right there.

"Shh, sweetheart," he soothed, holding me still by a hip as he slowly worked his cock into my ass. "Just the tip so far. You can take it. You're okay."

I was, but I already felt stretched wide from the thickness of his cock. I felt stretched wider as he pushed in deeper, and with a popping sensation, made it past the ring keeping him out.

"Ah yeah, so goddamn tight," he groaned, laying his front over my back and dropping a kiss on my neck. "We've got a ways to go. Deep breaths for daddy."

And then he slid in, deeper and deeper, waking up nerve endings I'd never known existed. As they came to life, so did I, the sensation of him in my ass and his murmured praise in my ear, *good girl* and *you feel so fucking gorgeous like this* making my nipples go tight and my clit pulse with pleasure. Still, pain radiated from my ass, my body protesting the pressure as he kept tunneling inside me without pause.

I keened from the confusing, topsy-turvy feeling where hurt and heaven intersected, and he laughed.

"We're only about halfway there, troublemaker. Relax for daddy now, I promise it's going to feel so good."

"It hurts, daddy," I whined.

"I know, sweetheart, I know. Shhh, you can do this for me, can't you? You like to make daddy's cock feel good, don't you? You're being such a good girl, and—" he groaned, "we're almost—" another groan, "—there."

With that he sighed, his balls resting against my ass cheeks.

"That's so good. You're so good, taking all of me. How does it feel?"

"Tight," I said.

"Yeah," he agreed, voice low with lust.

"Full," I added.

"Good. You should. You should feel so full that when I'm not inside you, you feel like something's missing."

He rested there a bit, quiet, and I rested with him too, even as a feeling built inside my ass, similar to the way my pussy felt when he stayed still inside me there, but different. Darker, hotter, confusingly good and bad at the same time. Without realizing it, I began to writhe under him, making him laugh.

"Yeah, you need me to fuck you now, don't you. I thought so. Just one second though, there's one more thing I need to do."

He reached over for something else, and then his hand was gripping mine, separating my fingers and slipping cool metal over my left ring finger.

My heart stuttered to a stop as I stared at the huge princess-cut diamond on my finger.

"Blake?" I asked, voice trembling.

"That's not what you call me when I'm inside you," he reminded me.

I ignored him. This was too monumental to call him daddy.

"Blake, what is that?"

He humphed. "Pretty sure that's an engagement ring."

I mean, yes. It was. But—

"You cannot propose to me with your dick up my ass!" I yelled.

He laughed. "Too bad, that's what I'm doing. I'm not asking, Lucy. I'm telling you, yes, with my cock nestled high in your tight little ass. You're going to marry me, and you're going to have my babies, and I'm going to fuck your pussy and your mouth and this tight little ass for the rest of your life. Say, 'yes, daddy.'"

"Blake," I protested—not at the proposal, but the circumstances of it.

He slapped my ass, hard.

"Say, 'yes, daddy,'" he repeated, his voice now low with warning.

I opened my mouth, and he shunted his hips even further forward. Before, I thought he'd been as deep as he could be. Before, I thought I'd felt full. Now, I felt him everywhere, and that pleasure-pain feeling spread, my ass clenching around him, as I squeaked:

"Yes, daddy."

"Perfect," he groaned, and I wasn't sure if it was my agreement to his proposal or the way I'd just squeezed his cock with my ass. "I love you, sweetheart," he said. "But now I'm going to fuck you hard and you're going to hold the fuck on while I do it."

He spread his hands over mine, holding me flat on the table, and withdrew slightly, only to push back in, slow at first, then faster and faster, as he repeated how much he loved me again and again, stirring my insides with his cock and adding a melting feeling to my stomach as my nipples got stiffer and my clit pulsed harder and I began to moan from how overwhelming the pleasure was.

"I love you so goddamn much, sweetheart," he said, his voice barely audible above his growl and rasp, as his hips slapped behind mine, powering into me over and over, his cock sliding over all those nerve endings and making my head spin. "I love you so fucking much, and what I'd really love is if you'd—ah, yeah, that's it, clench that ass around daddy's cock. That feels so fucking good, you have no idea."

My body basically melted against the desk, my toes curling in my shoes, as my pussy started clenching in time with my ass, an abyss looming in front of me, terrifying and exhilarating. I felt so good, so shockingly good, and I knew it wouldn't take much to send me deep into that unfamiliar territory.

All it took, in fact, was Blake saying, "Come for me, *little wife*, come hard," and pleasure erupted inside me and I must have screamed his name as I tumbled down, down, down. With a roar of my name, he followed me, shoving deep and bathing my insides with his hot cum.

Finally, he rested against my back, tugging my hair to turn my head so he could kiss me, sweetly and reverently, over and over.

I kissed him back, shaken to my core, literally.

Finally he stopped, asking me, "How was that?"

"I—I—I—"

He laughed.

"I never expected you to be at a loss for words."

"I don't know." I also laughed. "I guess that was amazing? It blew my mind for sure, I've forgotten how to think."

"Good." He kissed me again. "My fucking wife. God, that sounds so damn good, I want to fuck you all over again."

I protested with a whimper, and he promised, "When we

get home and get you cleaned up. But I don't want to neglect that mouth or your pussy, do I?"

"No, you don't," I sighed, as he pulled out of my ass, sending aftershocks through me, then lifted me up in his arms and carried me to his desk chair, placing me on his lap and stroking my hair, soothing me from the intensity of the experience.

I sighed, loving the way he loved me.

"I love you, Coach," I told him.

"I know, little troublemaker. But you can tell me every minute we're together for the rest of our lives if you want to. Because I plan on doing that for you."

And you know what?

That's exactly what he did.

>>>

Lucy's still causing trouble for Coach—and he loves every minute of it. Join my newsletter for a peek into their future: https://BookHip.com/HWCMQNW

>>>

Lucy and Coach appear in *Butterfly:* a dark college hockey romance where Leslie, Lucy's best friend, and Mason, one of Coach's players, fight, fuck, and fall in love—even though they're stepsiblings. <u>Read it now:</u> https:// books2read.com/butterflydarkhockey
And if you're reading the ebook, you can flip the page to read the prologue!

>>>

The men of Tabb U's rival team, the Reina U Kings, have their own, very, very dark romances. See how these possessive, obsessive, absolutely unhinged hockey players fall in love—with strong, determined women who don't go down without a fight.

Read *Brutal Game* now: https://books2read.com/brutalgame

Read *Heartless Game* now: https://books2read.com/heartlessgame

Preorder book three now: https://books2read.com/RG

>>>

Want to discover how Micah—hacker and stalker extraordinaire—and his two best friends stalk and kidnap the woman they're obsessed with possessing? Read *You Can Follow Me* now: https://a.co/d/4WEobAc

>>>

The Tabb U Terrors will be back with Emory and the lit professor he can't get out of his head—or let go. For updates, join my newsletter: https://www.jobrenner.com/

>>>

Want to know more about me, and get publishing updates, sneak peeks, and other news? Join my newsletter: https://www.jobrenner.com/

>>>

My Facebook Group, Jo Brenner's Bar, is full of

troublemakers. Join the party (and get to vote on fun things): https://www.facebook.com/groups/650710479937604

>>>

And finally, reviews make all the difference to an author's career. If you loved *Troublemaker*, review it here!

ACKNOWLEDGMENTS

I don't know, y'all. Being an author can be lonely, and I'm fortunate enough to have people in my life who make it less so, so I'm gonna thank them.

Boss Mommy: Sometimes I'm not sure who's in charge, but regardless, I am so grateful for the work you do for me. Thank you.

Emily: Thank you for understanding where a comma goes, pointing out what is and isn't physically possible, and just generally making me sound better.

Kenya: If it weren't for you, I'd still be spiraling and crashing out about not being able to start or complete everything. Thank you for always getting me to stop overthinking and start writing. I don't know what I'd do without you. Love you, friend.

Mikaela: You keep me pushing toward my goals, and also *always* give me an outlet to vent about whatever I need to vent about. Thank you so much for being my friend, you superhuman who continues to amaze me.

Brittney: How dare you live so far away from me! Not forgiven, and I expect a trip back to Edinburgh as an apology.

(P.S.: Everyone else, you have Brittney to thank for Coach taking Vice like a shot of Malört.)

O'Junea and Liz: This is the best I can do.

(I'm kidding. Love you both so much.)

To my alpha/beta team: Amoy, Liz, LeeAnne, Justine G,

Justine Y, Bekah, Madison, Kendra, and Michelle: Y'all are my champions. Y'all keep me motivated. And y'all make every single one of my books better. Thank you.

(Extra thanks to Justine G for the amazing stickers and for pointing out where my hockey went wrong and helping me make it right. If I screwed anything up, that's all on me, not her.)

To my Patreon Soulmates: Tabbie, Michele, Alicia, Meredith, Kirstie, and Kendra. I cannot begin to express how fucking grateful I am to each and every one of you for supporting me on this journey, for your input and insights, and your cheerleading. It means everything. Thank you.

To my ARC Team, Influencer Team, and Hype Team: Y'all are my troublemakers, my little badasses, my little furies. Y'all are everything. The fact that you care enough about my books and me to shout about them to the world is...I really don't have words to explain what it means to me. I love you all very very much.

And finally, as always, thank you to my readers. My entire life, all I dreamed about was telling stories: I never imagined so many people would want to read them. This world can be a tough fucking place; life can be tougher. But every time I sit down to write, on the good days and the bad, I think of you, on the other side of this, reading my words and loving my stories and coming back for more, and it helps me create them, one word at a time. Thank you isn't a strong enough phrase to describe how grateful I am, but it's what I've got, so—thank you.

Printed in Dunstable, United Kingdom

72086609R10170